--- ★ ---

I knew Augusta planned to attend the service Sunday and was looking forward to the music. I hoped she wouldn't be disappointed.

Cissy took her place at the great pipe organ, and the first few bars of "Hark, the Herald Angels Sing" resounded through the empty sanctuary. I felt a thrill as I always do at the joy and excitement of it, and took a deep breath to begin.

Ahead of me Idonia took one step into the sanctuary. *Glory to the newborn king!* we sang. And then somebody screamed. It had to be a soprano, because it was shrill enough to shatter glass, and it seemed to go on forever.

And—oh, God, it was Ellis!

--- ★ ---

Mignon F. Ballard

Hark!
The Herald Angel
Screamed

W☉RLDWIDE®

TORONTO • NEW YORK • LONDON
AMSTERDAM • PARIS • SYDNEY • HAMBURG
STOCKHOLM • ATHENS • TOKYO • MILAN
MADRID • WARSAW • BUDAPEST • AUCKLAND

Recycling programs
for this product may
not exist in your area.

HARK! THE HERALD ANGEL SCREAMED

A Worldwide Mystery/December 2010

First published by St. Martin's Press, LLC

ISBN-13: 978-0-373-26733-0

Printed in U.S.A.

For my readers, with thanks and appreciation

ONE

"LUCY NAN, ARE YOU sure we're on the right road?" my cousin Jo Nell asked. "Seems like we've been driving an awfully long time."

"Mama said the church was outside of Winnsboro," I told her, "and this *is* outside of Winnsboro, isn't it?"

"I'm sure she didn't mean this far outside. We must be half-way to Columbia by now and I haven't seen one sign of a small white church with a stone wall around it."

My cousin sat ramrod straight beside me in the same black wool suit she's been wearing for at least twenty years. Jo Nell never gains an ounce—the rat! On one bony knee she balanced a box holding her "Joyed-It" jam cake made from our grandmother's special recipe and so named because when anyone ate it they always said they "joyed-it." In her other hand my cousin clutched the black leather purse she carries every day from September through March. Sighing, she shifted the cake on her lap. "We should've turned left back there like I told you. Funeral's going to be over before we get there."

"You didn't tell me to turn *left*, you said turn *right*. This is Old Grange Road, isn't it? Here's an intersection coming up. Hurry, look and see what the sign says."

At the request of my mother, Jo Nell and I were on our way to the funeral of a relative, Mercer Vance, who was our second cousin or first cousin once removed. I never can get that straight.

My parents live in a condominium a couple of hundred miles away in Mount Pleasant, South Carolina, and pleasant it is, but it isn't a mountain at all but an island off the coast of Charleston.

"Mercer was my favorite cousin when we were growing up and I hate it that I can't be there," Mama told me, "but it's hard for your daddy to get around after his knee surgery and I don't feel right about leaving him." She gave me a chance for that to sink in. "You really don't mind going, do you, sugar—as a favor for your poor decrepit mother who suffered through twenty-seven hours of labor to bring you into the world?"

Although she's nearly eighty, my mother swims almost every day and plays golf at least once a week. I laughed. "Do spare me, please! Of course I'll go, but it's been years since I've seen some of those relatives and I can never remember who's who."

My family never let go of a name. Most of the men all the way back to Genesis were named Grayson, Mercer, or Vance while the women passed around Julia, Virginia, Lucinda, and Nellie. I'm named for my grandmother, who was named for her great-great-grandmother Lucinda Vance, who in 1835 with her husband, Mercer, built the columned home they named Willowbrook on the outskirts of my hometown of Stone's Throw, South Carolina. My grandmother was born there and lived there most of her life, but Mimmer's been gone for twenty years and except for some off and on tenants, the house has been empty since. Jo Nell claims it's haunted.

Now my cousin leaned forward shading her eyes to read the road sign as the pale November sun glinted off her bifocals. "I told you we were on the right road, Lucy Nan! Old Grange Road—plain as day—right there on that sign we just passed."

"Jo Nell Touchstone, you never told me any—"

"And there it is—white church with a stone wall. That's got to be it right up ahead…see it? *Slow down,* Lucy Nan! You're about to pass it." Jo Nell unbuckled her seat belt before we came to a complete stop. "Lord, I hope they haven't already said the benediction."

I parked and looked around as we wove through the rows of cars to the front of the church where two somber men waited. "Did you see a sign anywhere?" I asked. "I hope we're in the right place. Are you sure this is Capers Methodist Chapel?"

Jo Nell tramped ahead, pocketbook swinging from her arm. "What else can it be? Hurry, they're already singing a hymn."

I hurried. We were just in time for the last stanza of "In the Sweet By and By" when we took our seats in the next to the last pew.

I nodded politely to the people on either side of me, neither of whom I knew. They nodded back. It was close in the small sanctuary and heat blasted from a vent nearby. Jo Nell loosened the scarf around her neck and fanned herself with the memorial program. "Can you see Cudin' Grayson and them up front?" she whispered. "I don't see anybody I know."

"It's been so long I'm not sure I would recognize Cudin' Grayson if I saw him," I said, "but I'm pretty sure that's Mercer under all those flowers down there."

"Lucy Nan!" Jo Nell's eyes widened. "For goodness' sake—"

"Shh!" I said primly. "I think they're getting ready to start."

The minister mopped his face and stood. He wore a black robe and a stole as red as his glistening face and took a long drink of water before he opened the Bible to read the Twenty-third Psalm. His voice was low and soothing and I tried to picture myself in a shady green pasture where not-so-still waters rippled over mossy stones. Pausing at the end, he closed the Good Book softly, gave it a loving pat, and set it aside.

"Our good friend Lizzie Frye has left us for a better place," he began.

Lizzie Frye? What does she have to do with the price of eggs in China? I thought.

A lot, I soon discovered when I looked at the program. It was Lizzie Frye, not our cousin Mercer, under all those flowers down front.

Too late I glanced at the words on the hymnal in the rack in front of me: *Presbyterian Hymns*. We were in the wrong church!

Beside me Jo Nell leaned forward in the pew as if she couldn't believe her ears while the minister extolled the many virtues of the late Lizzie Frye. A faithful wife, loving mother, and dedicated church worker, she was especially noted for her generosity with homemade pepper jelly and watermelon rind pickles.

"We've gotta get out of here!" Jo Nell whispered to me from behind her program.

I made a face and shook my head. It was too late now. We couldn't just get up and walk out in the middle of a funeral service. Besides, someone else was stepping up to the pulpit to eulogize the departed. It turned out to be her daughter who was followed by another. Fortunately she had only two. Lizzie seemed like such a likable, down-to-earth sort of person, I was sorry I hadn't known her. Apparently so was Jo Nell as she sniffed a couple of times during the recessional hymn and blotted her eyes with a lace-trimmed hankie.

"I'm so sorry," I said to the family gathered outside as we filed from the church. And I *was* sorry, but I was also in a hurry. If we could just get away in time maybe Jo Nell and I could still get to poor Cousin Mercer's funeral before they put him in the ground.

Jo Nell, however, felt it her duty to extend her sympathy to each and every one, and when one of the family members responded with a hug, my cousin broke into tears. "Gone but not forgotten," she sobbed as I led her away. "She's going to be missed."

"And so are we if we don't make it to the right funeral," I told her. "Save some of those tears for Mercer, will you?"

As it turned out, we *were* on the right road but had been going in the wrong direction—which was entirely my cousin's fault, but I wasn't going there.

Capers Chapel, we were told, was about five miles down the road in the direction we had come and we got there just as the mourners lined up to follow the hearse to the cemetery. Jo Nell and I fell in behind them.

"No need to say anything about the extra memorial rites," I said later as we gathered around the grave site. "Maybe they'll think we've been here all along."

Nodding, Jo Nell agreed. "I guess what they don't know won't hurt them," she said. "I just hope we can get home before dark. I don't want to get lost out here again."

Of course Cousin Grayson and his wife Angela insisted that we come to the house after the service and I was glad for a chance to visit with my relatives inside where it was warm. It was the last week in November and sunlight was fading fast as we walked back to our cars from the cemetery. I hadn't seen Grayson and Angela ("my sweet angel," he calls her) since they were in Stone's Throw for my husband's funeral over four years earlier, but I was in such a zombie state at the time I barely remember their being there. Charlie was killed in a traffic accident while on a business trip and the shock of it turned my heart and my life inside out and upside down for a long time after that.

Augusta has helped me come to terms with losing Charlie as well as with several other of life's major bumps—such as murder—in what was once our peaceful little town. I must admit I had my doubts when she first showed up on my doorstep in her voluminous emerald cape, but there was something so right about her, something so good, I soon invited her into my life. I haven't regretted it. Augusta Goodnight is a guardian angel—*my* guardian angel she tells me, but sometimes she seems to end up watching out for most of my friends as well.

It was a pity she wasn't around that day, I thought, to steer us to the right funeral.

"Come and sit with me and tell me all about that grandson of yours. How old is he now?" Grayson's daughter, Nellie Virginia, said as we helped ourselves to the buffet on the dining room table. It seemed as if their friends and neighbors had brought enough food for the whole town and I was having trouble deciding between baked ham and fried chicken. I took some of both. Jo Nell's "Joyed-It" cake, I noticed, was going fast.

Nellie Virginia will be forty-seven in March—ten years younger than I am, and I always thought of her as a little sister following me like a shadow at family reunions. With little encouragement it didn't take me long to light into my favorite subject, my six-year-old grandson, Teddy. But when Nellie Virginia's eyes began to glaze over, I knew it was time to change the subject or shut up.

"Sorry," I said. "I should give people a buzzer or something so they can let me know my time's up."

My cousin laughed. "One of these days I'll probably be the same." She glanced at her young son Vance Tate, who was in deep conversation with Grayson, his grandfather, at the far end of the room. "And from the way things look, I might not have too long to wait."

I had been introduced earlier to Vance's girlfriend, Jamie, a willowy blonde, who now stood sipping wine with Angela and several of her friends in the living room.

"Oh? Is a wedding imminent? Vance was hardly more than a child when he came with you to Roger's wedding. Has it really been that long?" It was hard to believe our son and his wife Jessica would soon be celebrating their tenth anniversary.

"Believe it or not he'll be graduating from law school in June." She glanced at her son with a secret smile. "And it wouldn't surprise me one bit if he gave Jamie a ring for Christmas."

Jo Nell joined us with her plate piled high and began

buttering a couple of what had to be homemade yeast rolls. "I know I shouldn't have rice casserole and candied sweet potatoes, too, but I just couldn't resist," she said, digging into the latter.

"I hate you, Jo Nell," I mumbled under my breath.

"That was such a lovely service," Nellie Virginia said later over dessert. "I think Uncle Mercer would have approved, don't you?"

Jo Nell, who had just taken a bite of pecan pie, suddenly went into a coughing fit and had to leave the table.

Nellie Virginia rose to follow her. "Is she all right?"

"I think she'll be fine," I assured her. "Emotional, you know." Thank goodness she didn't bring up the subject of Cousin Mercer's service again.

After about an hour Jo Nell began looking at her watch every few minutes so I knew it was time to go. My cousin hates to be on the road long after dark.

"I suppose things are all right out at Willowbrook," Grayson said as we prepared to leave. "I know I should get out there more than I do, but Preacher Dave does a pretty good job looking after things."

My great-grandfather left Willowbrook to Mimmer's brother Sonny, who didn't want to live there and was glad to have her stay and look after the place. My mother and Jo Nell's were both born there. When Sonny died a few years after Mimmer, Willowbrook went to his sons, Mercer and Grayson. Mercer never seemed interested in the property, but a couple of years ago our cousin Grayson decided he'd try his hand at long-distance farming. He bought a small herd of Hereford cattle, had several acres planted in pines, and hired Dave Tansey, a jackleg preacher, to keep an eye on things.

Preacher Dave and his wife Louella live in a cottage on the place with their grown son, Jeremiah. I'd never met his wife and son, but Preacher Dave had recently taken a job filling in for the sexton at our church, Stone's Throw Presbyterian, after

Luther, our longtime maintenance man, fell and broke his hip replacing a light bulb. He seems to be doing a pretty good job because Pete Whittaker, our minister, says Dave even polished the brass lamp in his study that Luther had ignored for years.

I was almost out the door before I remembered to ask about the tree. Our church has been cutting a large cedar tree from Willowbrook for about as long as I can remember. It goes up in the fellowship hall the first week in December, and "angel" gifts for needy families are collected underneath the tree to be distributed in time for Christmas.

"Of course you can cut a tree! Cut as many as you like. You don't have to ask me," Cousin Grayson said. "I wish my sweet angel here would let us have one," he whispered loud enough for his wife to hear. "Nothing smells like Christmas like a real live evergreen, but she insists on putting up that artificial thing she ordered from some catalog."

"He's not the one who has to sweep up after it," Angela said, giving her husband her long-suffering look. "But you know you're always welcome to cut what you want."

"Want to drive out to Willowbrook with me to pick one out next week?" I asked Jo Nell as we started home. "Preacher Dave said he'd cut it down and take it to the church if we'll show him what we want. And we can get some greenery for the Advent wreath while we're there so Opal won't have an excuse to use that tacky plastic thing."

Opal Henshaw has taken it upon herself to be the unofficial chairperson of the decorating committee at Stone's Throw Presbyterian and everybody, including me, is too chicken to suggest somebody else.

"I don't like going out to Willowbrook," Jo Nell said, holding her hands to the heater.

"Why not?"

"Makes me sad to see it empty and neglected like that.

Mimmer loved that place so. I'm glad she can't see it now. Besides, you know it's haunted."

"We're just going to pick out a tree," I reminded her. "We won't be going inside. And you know very well all that talk about poor Celia is a lot of hooey."

Almost 150 years ago young Celia Vance was supposed to have thrown herself from the balcony at Willowbrook after her fiancé was killed in the battle at Manassas Gap. Mimmer claimed you always knew when Celia was around because you began to hear music and smell gardenias. They were Celia's favorite flowers, and according to our grandmother she was said to have been an accomplished violinist. Mimmer liked a good story.

"Hooey or not, you won't catch me out there," Jo Nell said. "Now, for heaven's sake, Lucy Nan, don't miss the turn up there and get us lost like you did coming over here."

TWO

"THAT TREE OVER THERE looks nice," Augusta said.

"Too skinny." Ellis Saxon frowned and shook her head. "You can see right through it."

I stopped to untangle my sleeve from a blackberry briar. "Here's a nice fat one—smells good, too."

Ellis inspected it closely. "No way. Double trunk. Keep looking."

The three of us were on a mission at Willowbrook to find the perfect Christmas tree for our church fellowship hall and so far nothing had met with Ellis's approval.

With a few exceptions, my friend Ellis is the only person besides me who can see and speak with Augusta. As the angel explained when she first appeared at my front door at 101 Heritage Avenue, Ellis could use a little looking after as well. And didn't *that* turn out to be true!

Augusta wrapped her voluminous green cape about her and shivered. She has never gotten over that treacherous winter with General Washington at Valley Forge. A host of heavenly help was on hand during those times, she tells me, but she has suffered from the cold ever since.

"Why don't you wait for us in the car?" I suggested. "We shouldn't be much longer." But Augusta had already disappeared behind a clump of cedars until all I could see was the gleam of her candle-bright hair as she moved among the branches.

The ground had been covered with frost when we first arrived, and now at mid-morning grass still crunched underfoot. Even in thick socks and my old clodhopper boots my feet were beginning to feel numb and I beat my gloved hands together to keep them warm.

"With it being this cold so early in December, maybe we'll have a white Christmas," I said.

"Remember that big snow when we were in the fourth grade?" Ellis said. "We slid down that hill behind the school on cafeteria trays, and I almost got hit by a car when mine ran into the street because I didn't know how to stop."

"How could I forget?" I said. "You scared me half to death."

"I was so terrified I couldn't think straight until you hollered at me to roll off—probably saved my life."

"Just remember that when Teddy comes around selling gift wrap for his class this year," I reminded her. "And for goodness' sake, will you please hurry and decide on a tree before my feet freeze to the ground!"

"I believe I see one over here!" Augusta called. "Come and look. What do you think?"

"I've already looked over there, Augusta. I didn't see a single one taller than I am." But Ellis plodded after her, holding aside limbs for me to follow.

"Now, where did *that* come from?" Ellis stopped so suddenly I almost stepped on her heels. "It's—it's perfect, but I'll swear it wasn't here earlier."

The lofty cedar lifted its feathery branches in majestic splendor over all the others around it. I pinched the tip of a frond to release a fragrance like Christmas perfume. "This one's just right," I said. "Hurry and tag it, Ellis, so we can collect the greenery we need and go home." I had already made note of a smaller cedar I'd seen that would be perfect for that spot in our living-room window, but we could come back for that later.

I looked around for Augusta, who stood quietly in the background. "Lucky you saw this one, Augusta. It should be a big hit at the church."

Ellis tied a strip of yellow ribbon to a branch of the tree so

Preacher Dave could find it. "It's the strangest thing! I don't understand why I didn't see it before."

"I think I know why," I told her, noticing Augusta's secret little smile. "It's because it wasn't there."

With a stroke of her fingers, the angel gave the elegant tree a parting caress. "Of course it was," she said. "It just grew a bit." With graceful steps she hurried along beside us in dainty fur-trimmed boots, her radiant hair escaping from a purple-tasseled hat. "And I believe I will wait for you in the car if you don't mind."

"Of course," I said, concerned. "Augusta, are you feeling all right?"

She smiled. "Fit as a banjo. Take your time."

Ellis rolled her eyes and grinned over the angel's choice of words. Augusta sometimes gets her expressions a little bit jumbled. "Why didn't you give her the keys so she can warm up the car?" she asked as we watched Augusta walk away.

"She won't use them," I said. "Augusta's never been comfortable with the internal combustion engine—says she much prefers a horse."

Ellis laughed. "She seems quite at home with other modern conveniences like the refrigerator, for instance, and the washing machine, and I know better than to interrupt when she's watching those old movies on TV."

"But she still practically jumps through the ceiling when I turn on the garbage disposal," I said, smiling at the thought. Augusta had come to my house the year before when I advertised a room for rent in our local paper, and although she has served as a guardian angel "temp" from time to time throughout the ages, she's just now becoming accustomed to some of our more recent inventions.

I skirted a scattering of pine saplings as we made our way to the house. Willowbrook reminded me of a once proud lady who had met with unfortunate times and was in dire need of a visit to the beauty parlor, or better still, a good plastic surgeon.

The old house looked bare and forlorn standing in scruffy undergrowth with sagging shutters and peeling paint. Jo Nell had a point. I was glad Mimmer couldn't see it now.

"There's a holly tree by the portico around front," I said, "and there should be plenty of hemlock and pine on the other side of the house."

"Maybe we'll see the ill-fated Celia," Ellis said. "Isn't that where she was supposed to have fallen?"

"Or jumped." I stopped to break off a few branches of pine, making certain to choose the ones with the prettiest cones. "Remember that poem we made up about her?"

Ellis laughed. "Poor Celia! Weren't we the callous lot—you, Joel, and me? I think your mother got kind of upset with us."

"But not Mimmer! In fact it was her idea," I said.

My great-grandmother Nellie had written a verse about Celia sometime in the early nineteen hundreds and it had even been published in *The Messenger,* our local weekly, which must have been having a light news week at the time. Mama kept a copy of it in her scrapbook, and much to her dismay my brother, Joel, came across it and delighted in quoting it on every occasion while I fluttered in the background in an old window curtain.

Now, striking a pose, I touched my palm to my chest and chanted:

"When there's music in the air
You'll see Celia standing there.
Quietly now she moves in grace,
Soft the smile upon her face.
Then, like a shadow, Celia's gone,
But the scent of flowers lingers on."

Ellis responded by climbing on a convenient tree stump to echo the parody the three of us had collaborated on years before:

"Did Celia jump or did she fall
When she landed in a sprawl?
Or maybe someone gave a push
To send her tumbling on her tush.
Poor Celia! What a sad demise!
It must have been a big surprise,
At least I think it would to most
To have to end up as a ghost."

I laughed. "Well, I hope she's not around today. It's cold enough out here without ectoplasm."

"We'd better hurry before Augusta turns into an icicle," Ellis said, adding more evergreens to her bag. "How much holly do you think we'll need?"

But I didn't answer because either somebody had dumped a scarecrow on the porch beneath the balcony or poor Celia had jumped again.

"HURRY! GET AUGUSTA," I said—or tried to say, but the words came out in a squawk. And it wasn't necessary anyway because suddenly Augusta was standing there beside us.

Ellis dropped the greenery she had collected. "Is he still breathing? Do you know who it is?"

The man lay on his stomach with his legs bent beneath him in the center of the porch between two Doric columns, and from the peculiar angle of his head, it looked as if his neck had been broken. I knelt and felt for a pulse, finding none, while Augusta checked for breathing. She looked at me and shook her head. "Maybe you should give him artificial insemination," she said.

"In his case I don't think that would do any good," I told her, realizing what she meant. "I'm afraid he's beyond help now."

"My phone's in the car. I'll call nine-one-one!" Ellis took off running, but we both knew it was too late to help the man sprawled on the portico at Willowbrook.

"He's still warm. It must have just happened," I told Augusta. "Looks like he fell from the balcony up there. The railing's broken."

"Do you know who he is?" Augusta touched the man's face as if in a silent benediction, her eyes filled with compassion.

"Never saw him before," I said. The dead man, dressed in faded jeans and a tan jacket, was stocky and seemed to be of medium height. His dark curly hair was badly in need of a trim and he had the beginnings of a beard.

"Oh, dear God!" I stepped back as it occurred to me that this might be Preacher Dave's son.

"The man who looks after this place has a grown son who lives with them but I've never seen him. Do you suppose this might be Jeremiah Tansey?"

"Do you know his age? This fellow looks to be in his late twenties or perhaps his early thirties." Augusta stooped to examine him more closely.

I considered searching the man's pockets for some kind of identification but couldn't bring myself to do it. We would find out soon enough anyway, I thought, as Ellis returned to tell us the police and an ambulance were on the way.

Stepping back, Augusta looked up at the balcony. "Why don't you keep an eye on things here? I believe I'll step inside for a minute."

"Keep an eye on what? He isn't going anywhere." Ellis hugged herself for warmth. "And it isn't any warmer in there than it is out here."

"We can't get in anyway," I said. "The house is always kept locked to discourage vandals."

I knew of course that wouldn't deter Augusta but didn't take to the idea of being left here with the dead man while both of us grew colder by the minute.

And neither did Ellis. "Why do you want to go inside?" she asked, slowly backing away from the house and the body that lay beside it. "There's nothing in there to see."

"He must have gotten in somehow or else how did he manage to fall from the balcony?" Augusta said. "And, as you can see, the front door is slightly ajar. Perhaps whoever was with him is still in there."

"What makes you think someone was with him?" I asked, glancing up at the shadowy balcony. But Augusta had already slipped inside.

Through the glass panels on either side of the heavy door I glimpsed peeling wallpaper and layers of grime on the sturdy old heart-of-pine floors, which were in sharp contrast to the elegant gold acanthus leaves on the hallway arch as well as on the ceiling medallion in what was once the drawing room. Years ago Joel and I had played hide-and-seek under the graceful curving stairway. I was not going inside that house—angel or no angel!

"What if there *is* somebody in there?" I said, joining Ellis in the yard.

"If there is, Augusta will let us know, but what would anybody be doing in there?" She glanced briefly at the still form beneath the balcony. "What was *he* doing in there?"

"I don't know unless he turns out to be Jeremiah Tansey," I said.

Ellis frowned. "Is that Preacher Dave's son?"

"Right. Lives with his parents in the Green Cottage over there."

The Green Cottage where the caretaker lives was now painted more of a pale yellow and hadn't been green since I was a child, but old habits die hard here in Stone's Throw. I still refer to most of my high school classmates by their maiden names and some of them have been married for almost forty years.

But Ellis shook her head. "Nope. Dave's son is fair and kind of skinny—not nearly as large as this man. I saw him when he helped his dad hang those new curtains in the ladies' parlor at the church. This man isn't Jeremiah Tansey."

"Thank God for that!" I said, relieved that we wouldn't have to be the bearers of sad news to Preacher Dave and his wife, Louella. But then the dead man was somebody's son or husband or brother and I felt ashamed of myself for being so grateful. Must be Augusta's influence.

Ellis was still for a minute. "Lucy Nan, do you hear that music?"

"What music?"

She cocked her head. "For a second I thought I heard violin music—you know—like Celia was supposed to have played."

"No, and I don't smell gardenias, either," I told her. "What you probably hear is a siren. Here comes an ambulance now, and finally the police."

Although Willowbrook had been a country estate in my grandmother's day, and even in my mother's, the city limits of Stone's Throw had eventually crept out to include it.

Captain Alonzo Hardy of the Stone's Throw Police Department stopped in mid-stride when he saw me. "*You*!" he said, shoving back his cap to reveal his fiery red hair. He didn't look happy to see me, but I didn't take offense because I was certainly glad to see him.

"Captain," I said, going to meet him. I was relieved to see he was accompanied by my friend Kemper Mungo instead of that nincompoop Police Chief Elmer Harris. During the recent troubles at the local college I learned I would much rather have Sergeant Mungo on my side than against me.

"Any idea who this man might be or what he was doing out here?" the captain asked after a preliminary look at the dead man.

I shook my head. "None. Could be a vagrant looking for a place to get in out of the cold."

Kemper glanced up at the splintered balcony railing. "Looks like he might've had a little too much to drink last night."

Ellis approached with an armful of pine that filled the air with its clean fresh scent. "There's no way it could've happened last night," she told him. "He was still warm when we found him."

"And when was that?" Captain Hardy asked.

"About fifteen minutes ago," I said. "We were gathering greenery for the Advent wreath—"

"And were about to clip some holly from this tree right here when we saw him," Ellis pointed out as she shook one of the lower limbs of the evergreen.

"I don't suppose you saw or heard anyone else around here?" the captain asked as Kemper roped off the area.

Ellis, who had been busily adding holly to her collection, looked quickly at an upstairs window. "No, but…"

"But what?" he asked, squinting against the late morning sun.

Ellis avoided looking at me but I knew what she was thinking. *Augusta might have seen something when she went inside the house.*

"The Tanseys live over there in the Green—I mean the yellow house a little way down the road," I said. "Dave Tansey sort of looks after this place. Maybe they'll know something about him."

Kemper frowned. "Tansey. That Jeremiah's folks?"

"That's right," Ellis told him. "You know him?"

"I know him," Kemper said. It didn't sound as if the two were on a friendly basis.

The captain gave Kemper a look that clearly read, *Keep your mouth shut.* "I expect we'll be finding out more about this fellow here before too long," he said, giving Ellis and me a dismissive nod as the coroner and a couple of police cars pulled into the yard behind him. "I think you've told us about all we need to know for now," he told us. "No reason for all of us to freeze out here—that is if you think you have enough holly there."

This last was directed at Ellis, who crammed one more limb

in her bulging bag. "We'll be in touch, and if anything comes to mind, you will let us know, won't you?"

ELLIS LOOKED OVER her shoulder the whole time as we walked back to where we had parked the car, bags of evergreens bumping along between us.

"If you're looking for Augusta you're wasting your time," I told her. "You know good and well she'll be waiting for us in the car."

And of course she was. We found her muffled from head to toe in a throw I keep for that purpose. "It's going to take about a pot of coffee to warm me up," Augusta said from the backseat. "Do you think you might get that heater going soon?"

Ellis and I didn't speak as we quickly crammed our fragrant gatherings into the trunk and drove away. Both of us were eager to put that dreadful scene behind us.

Ellis turned to Augusta as we entered the main road. "Well?" she said.

Augusta pulled her knitted hat closer about her ears. "Well, what?"

"Did you see or hear anybody when you went inside the house?" I could tell Ellis was trying to hide her exasperation.

But Augusta only shivered and drew her wrap more snugly about her.

"For heaven's sake, Augusta, tell us! You *did* see something, didn't you?" I caught her eye in the rearview mirror but she quickly looked away.

"I was so hoping it might snow," she said, scanning the sky. "Do you think it will?"

I glanced silently at Ellis, who shrugged. I could have told her that if Augusta Goodnight had anything to share she would tell us when she was good and ready, and not a second before.

THREE

"I'm going to have to quit hanging around with you—in fact, it makes me a little uncomfortable having you right next door," my neighbor Nettie McGinnis said.

Bellawood, the restored plantation where I work several days a week, was planning its annual Christmas candlelight tour and Nettie had brought over her punch bowl for the occasion.

"I'm sorry to hear that," I said. "How come?"

She set the box on my kitchen table and plopped into a chair. "How many bodies have you found in the last year or so? Three? Four? I've come to the conclusion it might be in my best interest to stay out of your way."

"I wasn't even there when that man fell from the balcony yesterday—cross my heart." And I did. "The police think he probably spent the night in there to get in out of the cold. It wouldn't be the first time somebody found a way inside Willowbrook. Preacher Dave tries to keep the place secure but he says he had to run off a couple of teenagers making out in there a few weeks ago."

Nettie frowned. "Preacher Dave? Isn't he the man the deacons hired to fill in for Luther at the church?"

"Right. He and his family have been living out there for over a year since Cudin' Grayson decided to try his hand at farming. Kinda looks after the place."

Nettie helped herself to one of Augusta's apple spice muffins as I poured coffee for both of us. I had known our neighbor for as long as I could remember, but when Charlie and I moved into the house on Heritage Avenue over twenty years ago she became an integral part of our lives. "This man who fell—do they know who he is—or should I say, *was*?" she asked.

"Kemper said they didn't find any kind of identification on him," I said. "They don't seem to know a lot more than they did."

"Had he been drinking?" Nettie stirred another spoonful of sugar into her brew.

"I guess they'll know more about that after they get the autopsy report. According to Kemper they found several empty beer cans and an old whiskey bottle or two upstairs but he didn't know if any of them belonged to the dead man. Preacher Dave said he could've sworn he locked that front door up tight but it wasn't closed when we saw it. Looks like he just walked right in and made himself at home."

My neighbor clicked her false teeth, a sign which usually meant she was studying on something. "How do they know he fell from that balcony? Could've been pushed, you know."

I passed her another muffin. "Or jumped like poor Celia. But why come all the way out to Willowbrook to do away with himself? Nobody here seems to have even known the man."

She chewed on that for a minute. "What about the preacher's son—Joshua, isn't it?"

"Jeremiah. His mother says no," I told her.

"Or that's what he would want her to believe, but I wouldn't put too much faith in what that boy says. Kim—you know Kim, does my hair at the Total Perfection—well, she says she's seen him hanging out with that rough bunch over at the Red Horse Café."

"What was Kim doing at the Red Horse Café?" I asked, but Nettie didn't bother to answer. "I don't reckon you all had a chance to get enough evergreens for the Advent wreath," she said.

"Then you reckon wrong," I told her. "Geraldine Overton is working on it as we speak. Says she'll keep it in that big refrigerator at the church until Sunday." Geraldine Overton used to work part time at a flower shop.

"You could do just as good a job as Geraldine," Nettie told me. "Back when you used to help out at Bud's Blooms I thought you made some lovely arrangements, Lucy Nan."

I laughed. "My children called them 'derangements,'" I said. "Besides, I don't want to risk the wrath of Opal Henshaw. She's already on the warpath about our using fresh greenery."

"Opal's always got her drawers in a wad about something," Nettie said, lifting the punch bowl from its box. "Do you think this is gonna be big enough?"

"If it was any bigger we could swim in it," I said. "But I'd hate it if anything happened to your pretty cut-glass bowl, Nettie. Are you sure you want to let us borrow this?"

"Cut glass, nothing! I got that old thing at the Five and Ten Cent Store for three ninety-eight back when I was first married. Tell 'em they can keep it if they want. I can't remember the last time I used it."

Nettie blew off my attempt at thanks. "What are they going to serve?"

"Just a few simple things: shortbread cookies, ginger-bread, orange-cranberry punch, and peppermint sticks for the children."

My neighbor snorted. "What? No syllabub? I was always told that's what they used to serve for Christmas, weddings, and almost any festive occasion. Every house worth its salt had a syllabub churn."

"So does Bellawood," I said. "I've seen one in the kitchen, but that's kind of like eggnog, isn't it? Lord, Genevieve Ellison would have a cow if we brought alcohol onto the property!" Genevieve, a strict teetotaler, was on the board of directors at Bellawood and I wanted to keep my job. I had been hired to take care of publicity and public relations for the plantation over a year ago, and although the pay wasn't anything to brag about, I could take care of much of the work from home.

"They've asked The Thursdays to help greet visitors," I told her. "I think you and Jo Nell are supposed to be in the schoolhouse."

"Well, I hope they'll have a fire in that old stove out there. I just about froze my ass off that year they stuck me in the upstairs hall." She frowned. "Where are you going to be?"

"Entrance hall, I think. Of course I'll get a chill every time somebody opens the door. Lucky Ellis gets to help in the kitchen."

Two other members of our book club, The Thursday Morning Literary Society (which now meets on Monday afternoons), Idonia Mae Culpepper and Zee St. Clair, were scheduled to guide guests through the upstairs rooms. Our seventh and youngest member, Claudia Pharr, planned to attend a holiday program at her son's school and wouldn't be available to help out that night.

"Some of the schoolchildren plan to decorate a small tree with cranberries and popcorn for the parlor," I said. "I remember Mimmer helping us string those for our tree when I was a little girl."

"I'm glad your grandmamma can't see the sad condition her old home has fallen into," Nettie said with a sigh. "Grayson ought to be ashamed for not taking better care of that place—Mercer, too, God rest him. It's a wonder it hasn't burned to the ground."

"It was rented off and on for a while," I reminded her, "but the last tenants couldn't afford to heat those big rooms. You remember my cousin Nellie Virginia, don't you? Well, she told me her son Vance has shown an interest in Willowbrook, but of course he's young and has no idea how much it would cost to keep it up. His mother thinks he's crazy. Says he's got his head in the clouds because he's in love."

Nettie nodded. "Bless his heart, I hope his girlfriend has money."

My NEIGHBOR HADN'T BEEN gone five minutes when Ellis phoned. "Got something to tell you," she said.

"What?"

"Tell you when I get there. Just wait till you hear this! Need anything from the store? I have to stop by the market first."

"Why do you do this?" I asked. "You *always* do this, Ellis Saxon!"

"Do what?" Innocence dripped from her voice.

"You know very well what. You bait me with the promise of some tantalizing news, then leave me hanging while you go running—"

But I was talking to a dial tone. Ellis had hung up.

I was washing a handful of dishes a few minutes later when a gust of cold air ruffled the pages of a magazine on the kitchen table and Augusta, followed by our dog, Clementine, came in from their afternoon romp in the backyard. The magazine was one of those publications that featured an article on "How to Lose Ten Pounds in Ten Days" and a recipe for Christmas trifle with eggnog custard and whipped cream, both in the same issue. Augusta had seemed especially interested in the trifle.

"I do believe it's getting colder," she said, hurrying to warm her hands by the sitting room fire. "Must have dropped ten degrees since morning."

I followed her and curled up at one end of the sofa where Clementine reached up to nuzzle me with her frosty nose. "Colder than yesterday?" I asked. "I think I was almost as cold as you were while we waited for the police to come. I wonder if they ever found out what that man was doing at Willowbrook."

"I don't imagine it was for any good purpose," she said, turning to warm her angelic behind. "I'm afraid we haven't seen the end of the difficulties out there."

"Does that mean you saw something when you were inside?"

She added a stick of firewood to the blaze. "Not at all."

"Augusta Goodnight! You're every bit as exasperating as

Ellis! I do believe you're teasing me on purpose." I told her about Ellis's earlier telephone call.

"Lucy Nan, you must know by now that I dislike leaping to conclusions."

Augusta sat on the rug with the big dog's head in her lap and stroked the animal's ears. If Clementine had been a cat she would have purred. "If I had *seen* something I would have told you."

"Ah," I said. "But you *heard* something, didn't you?"

Augusta stared into the flames. Her long necklace of glittering stones reflected the blue and amber of the fire's blaze. "I'm not sure," she said finally.

"What do you mean you're not sure?"

"It could have been a mouse—and old houses do creak."

"What's this about a mouse? Should I jump up on a chair and scream?" Neither of us had heard Ellis enter by way of her usual route through the kitchen.

"It would take more than a mouse to make you scream," I told her. I had made up my mind I wasn't going to mention her earlier hint of news.

"We were referring to a noise I might have heard while I was inside the house at Willowbrook," Augusta explained. "It was rather like a…scuttling sound as if someone were trying to keep quiet."

"Could you tell where it was coming from?" I asked.

"I thought at first someone might be hiding in the room to the right of the stairway, but there was no one there," she said. "It was almost as if it came from inside the wall."

Ellis brightened. "Really? How exciting!"

I made room for Ellis on the sofa. "Mimmer used to say there was a secret stairway in there somewhere but she never would let us look for it. She pretended she didn't know where it was, but I'm sure she did. Said she was afraid the steps might be rotten and we would fall through."

"Well, whoever might have been there is probably gone now,"

Augusta said, "although I'm afraid we haven't heard the last of this. And I would hope your friends from the police will check to see if there really is a stairway there."

"Do you think they'll come back?" I asked.

"I suppose it all depends on what they were doing out there in the first place." Augusta gently dislodged Clementine from her lap and stood, shucking her serious tone. "At any rate, it's a bit early to worry about it just yet. Would anyone else like hot chocolate?"

Ellis waved her hand in the air. "I would! But doesn't anybody want to hear my news?"

I yawned. "What news?"

Ellis shrugged. "Well, if you really don't want to know…"

"Depends," I said. "Does it involve scandal, intrigue, or romance?"

Ellis grinned. "Romance."

"Whose? Yours?" I asked.

Ellis laughed. "Of course not! Bennett and I are *married*—not that we don't—oh, never mind! It's about Idonia," she said.

I think I gasped, but shame on me if I did. "Idonia? *Idonia Mae Culpepper*?"

Ellis nodded. "The very same."

Augusta stood in the middle of the room with her arms folded. "I don't understand. Why shouldn't your friend have love in her life?"

"Well, she should…could…I guess," I stammered while Ellis readily agreed. "Of course, of course," she said. "It's just that… Idonia…well…"

Augusta twined her necklace through her fingers. "Well, what?"

"It's just that she's *Idonia*," I admitted finally. "Actually Idonia was married briefly when she was a lot younger but it didn't work out. He turned out to be a rotten apple."

"An *apple*?" Augusta shook her head.

"Ran around on her," Ellis explained. "Rotten to the core. She's been kind of sour on men ever since."

Augusta paused in the doorway. "A sour apple…I see," she said, although I wasn't sure she did. "So what were you going to tell us?" she asked Ellis.

Ellis paused to get the full benefit of our attention. "Idonia has a gentleman friend," she announced.

"Really? Who? Anybody we know?" I asked.

"Does the name Melrose DuBois ring a bell?" she said.

"Should it?" I laughed. "You're kidding, aren't you? You made that up. Nobody is named Melrose DuBois!"

Ellis stood to follow Augusta into the kitchen. "Idonia's fellow is. Works part time for Al Evans over at the funeral home. I think he and Al are cousins or something."

I trailed along after them. Clementine trailed after me. "How do you know all this?" I asked.

"Opal Henshaw told me. He's taken a room with her at the Spring Lamb."

"God help him," I said. The Spring Lamb is a bed-and-breakfast, so called because of the two cement lamb planters filled with plastic flowers on either side of the front door. I hoped Idonia's friend didn't have a big appetite because he wouldn't get much to eat under that roof. Opal Henshaw could squeeze a nickel till the buffalo bellowed.

"When did all this come about?" I asked, adding a dollop of whipped cream to my hot chocolate. For some reason since Augusta arrived I've had trouble zipping my pants.

"Opal tells me he's been with them about a month," Ellis said. "I think he and Idonia met at Harris Teeter over a bunch of grapes. He asked her to help him pick out some fruit."

Probably to supplement the breakfast menu, I thought. "Romance in the produce department…sounds like the title of a book. Has Idonia said anything to you about him?"

Ellis sipped her hot drink slowly. "Not yet, but The Thursdays are meeting at my house Monday. What do you bet we get a full report then?" She closed her eyes. "Mmm…tastes like cinnamon in here. Augusta, this hot chocolate is heavenly."

Augusta smiled. "Of course it is," she said.

FOUR

ZEE ST. CLAIR FLUNG her crimson cloak over the back of Ellis's living room sofa and took a stance. The Thursdays had just
finished reading *Zelda*, a biography of Zelda Sayre Fitzgerald,
and Zee had been acting even more flamboyant than usual.
"I think we should have a caroling party for Christmas this
year," she announced, "instead of going out to dinner like we
always do."

Jo Nell, who had just settled comfortably in the wing chair
by the fireplace, sat up so suddenly she frightened Ellis's cat,
Cookie, who had been sleeping underneath. "You mean walk
around out in the cold and sing on neighbors' porches?"

"Why not?" Zee tossed her brightly tinted curls. "We used
to do it all the time. Remember what fun we had? We could
have a few glasses of wine before we start, then come back to
Lucy Nan's for a covered dish."

"Fine with me," I said, since it was my time to host
anyway.

Idonia looked thoughtful. "Would it be all right if I asked
Mel—" she began.

"I think it's a great idea!" Claudia Pharr set her steaming
cup of Russian tea on the marble-topped coffee table and took
a calendar from her purse. "When?"

"Would next week be too soon?" I asked. "We can work it in
between rehearsals for Lessons and Carols and the candlelight
tour at Bellawood…and by the way, I'm counting on some of
you to help us decorate out there."

Nettie said she'd be glad to help decorate and would even go along with the caroling if we would agree to carry her home in a pack saddle if her feet gave out.

I laughed. I had almost forgotten about the term we'd used as children for making a seat with four crossed arms.

"I think I'll be able to help, Lucy Nan, and I'd like to invite Melrose to join us for caroling if that's all right." Idonia spoke louder this time.

Zee nodded. "Of course—Melrose *who*?"

"Melrose DuBois—he's someone I've been seeing." Idonia sipped calmly from her cup but I noticed her hands shook slightly when she set it down.

And then the bombardment began: "Where did you meet him?"

"When did you start seeing him?"

"Is he from around here?"

"How long were you going to keep this from us, you sly fox?" Zee asked, perching on the arm of Idonia's chair. "Tell us, is he handsome? What's he like?"

"All right! Enough!" Idonia shook her head, laughing, and told us how she had met Melrose in the produce department at Harris Teeter. He had taken her to dinner twice and they had seen several movies together, she said, and until he could find a more permanent place, he was staying with Opal Henshaw at the Spring Lamb.

Her face flushed almost as red as her hair. "He's merely a friend," she stressed, "but it's nice to have someone to go out with—something to look forward to…and well…I find Melrose pleasant company."

"I think that's wonderful," I said, "and of course you should invite Melrose to the party. I plan to ask Ben as well."

Benjamin Maxwell and I had been seeing one another for over a year and it hadn't taken me long to learn that he was not only an extraordinary spinner of yarns, but sang a pretty good baritone as well.

"There are a lot of older people here in Stone's Throw—

especially in the neighborhoods right here in town—who might enjoy having carolers come by," Claudia said brightly.

Ellis passed around a tray of sandwiches. "In case you haven't noticed, we *are* the older people here in Stone's Throw," she informed her.

"I hope your friend won't have to stay at the Henshaw place long," Jo Nell said to Idonia. "That Opal Henshaw's queen of the skinflints—and fussy! Lord, everything has to be just so!"

Idonia smiled. "I think Melrose just tries to stay out of her way. He said once he accidentally brushed against a picture hanging on the wall and she about knocked him down to straighten it."

Ellis nodded. "Probably obsessive-compulsive."

"More like obsessive-*re*pulsive," Nettie said. "That woman gets on my last nerve."

"I think she's just plain bossy," I said. "Everything has to be Opal's way. I heard she practically had a fit and fell in it when she heard we were going to use fresh greenery in the Advent wreath this year."

Claudia shook her head. "I dread having to go with her on the fruitcake run," she said.

I laughed, picturing panicky people fleeing from giant fruit-cakes with legs. "Fruitcake run? I suppose you're running *from* them."

But Claudia waved my comment aside. "Every year our Sunday school class takes fruitcake and homemade cookies to shut-ins and we've always included Luther and his family, as well. Since Preacher Dave is filling in as sexton, we voted to take the Tanseys some, too."

"Lucky Tanseys," Ellis whispered under her breath.

"I always seem to get stuck on the committee with Opal," Claudia said with a groan. "I wish I could think of a good excuse not to go."

"Cheer up! Maybe you'll come down with smallpox or typhoid fever or something," Zee told her.

"Smallpox? My goodness, Zee. People don't get—" Claudia smiled as realization dawned. "Oh, you're pulling my leg again!" She shrugged. "Well, we're not going for another week so with luck I might catch a mild cold."

Nettie clicked her teeth in annoyance. "For heaven's sake, Claudia, just tell the woman you won't be able to help out that day."

Claudia paled. *"Tell Opal Henshaw that?"*

"Melrose is taking me to a choral concert at the college tonight," Idonia said, "and I'm having a terrible time deciding what to wear."

"Your black sheath always looks nice," Zee said. "Or what about that blue silk you bought last year?"

Ben and I had made plans to go to the concert, too, but I didn't want to steal Idonia's thunder by mentioning it. "You'd look great in either one," I told her, "but I kind of favor the blue."

"Will Julie be home for Christmas this year, Lucy Nan?" Jo Nell asked as we helped clear away teacups.

"For five whole days! She saved part of her vacation time and we're—I'm making new curtains to jazz up her room a little."

"You're making curtains?" Nettie didn't even bother to hide her amazement. She has never forgotten that clown costume I made for Teddy's third Halloween. I forgot to put an opening in the neck and he couldn't get his head through.

"Well, my goodness, it's not that big a deal!" I told her, not daring to look at Ellis, who knew who was *really* making the curtains.

"Or I could wear that turquoise pants suit I made last winter," Idonia mused aloud. "Melrose says that color shows off my hair."

Everyone agreed that the turquoise pants suit would be a good choice.

"Have you heard any more about what happened to that poor man you found out at your grandmother's old home?" Zee asked me as The Thursdays prepared to leave. She frowned. "You don't suppose somebody pushed him, do you?"

"If somebody did, the police aren't saying," I told her. "Kemper said they looked around inside but didn't see anything suspicious."

Idonia shrugged into her coat and tucked her purse and her book under an arm. "Well, I must be off if I'm to have my hair done this afternoon. Melrose doesn't like to be late."

"DID YOU TELL KEMPER about the secret stairway?" Ellis asked after the others had left.

"I left him a message but haven't heard back. He probably thinks I've let my imagination run away with me again."

"Again? What do you mean, *again*?" she snorted. "If they didn't have us to prod them along, the police here in Stone's Throw wouldn't have a clue!"

I had to admit she had a point.

"I guess you noticed Kemper didn't seem to think too much of Jeremiah Tansey," Ellis said. "I wonder if he had anything to do with all this."

"Nettie seems to think he runs around with that rough bunch at the Red Horse," I said, "but that doesn't mean he's a murderer."

"Hmm…I wonder if his dad knows he hangs around out there. Preacher Dave is as straitlaced as they come—or seems to be. I've never met Louella, though. Wonder what his wife's like."

"I don't know," I said, "but I'll soon find out. Grayson has ordered one of those huge Christmas baskets from that specialty shop over in Fort Mill and I told him I'd pick it up tomorrow and deliver it to the Tanseys. Says he feels kind of guilty because he hasn't done anything for them since they've been out there at Willowbrook."

"You're going to The Peach Stand? Wait up a minute, will you?" Ellis hurried away and returned with several bills that she stuffed into my hand. "How about bringing me a couple of jars of peach pickles and some blackberry jam?" She hesitated while I shoved the money into my purse. "You're not nervous about going out to Willowbrook again, are you? I'd go with you but Susan and I are shopping for the new baby tomorrow."

Ellis's daughter was expecting a boy after Christmas and Ellis's husband Bennett had already bought enough sports equipment to furnish a gym.

"Actually I'm kind of curious to see what Louella's like," I said. "Besides, Augusta's going with me."

"She was with us the other day when we found that body, too," Ellis reminded me. "You be careful out there, Lucy Nan."

THE GREEN COTTAGE sat about a quarter of a mile from the plantation house at the end of a long gravel road in a grove of oak trees that had been huge even when I was a child. In the pasture across the road reddish-brown and white cattle grazed, and beyond that a hill of new pine saplings showed green against the brown December landscape. A couple of Herefords licking a salt block looked at us briefly through the barbed-wire fence as we turned into the drive. "Have you noticed how cows always look bored?" I said.

Augusta laughed. "Wouldn't you be?"

A rambling pyracantha bush stretched arms full of fiery orange berries against the pale yellow walls of the house and browning chrysanthemums, once purple, tumbled against the doorstep. Someone—Louella, I presumed—had hung a wreath of gold-sprayed cotton bolls on the front door. I had seen some like it earlier at the craft fair at the Baptist Church.

Preacher Dave himself met me at the door. He was a tall man with thinning hair and stooped shoulders. Keen blue eyes smiled at me from a weathered face. "Come in, come in!" Accepting the basket, he stepped aside to usher me in front of him. "And excuse the coveralls, please. Just got through waxing floors over at the church and haven't had time to change."

"That's quite all right…I don't mean to stay…" I found myself seated in a comfortable overstuffed chair, the arms and back of which were protected with crocheted doilies. "My cousin Grayson asked me to drop this by to thank you for looking after the property. He plans to get up here himself soon after the holidays but wanted to wish you and your family a merry Christmas."

Preacher Dave set the large basket on the floor. "My goodness, this looks wonderful, but it isn't necessary…" His voice trailed as he examined the contents of ham, cheese, jams, and pickles. "Louella! Come here, honey, and see what Santa Claus brought us!"

"Are those spiced peaches? My favorites! What a nice surprise!" At first glance Louella Tansey seemed to be all of one color—sort of a faded tan. Her thin brownish hair was pulled back in what would've been a bun if there had been enough of it and her eyes, behind bifocals, seemed to take on the tone of the beige housedress she wore. The only bright color, I noticed, was the green rickrack trim on the woman's apron. "Louella Tansey," she said, offering her hand. "Let me get you something to drink. I just made tea."

"Thank you, but I can't stay," I said, introducing myself. "I know it must be close to your supper hour." Augusta, who stood by the upright piano across the room, brightened at the mention of tea, but I could have told her it was probably iced tea our hostess was offering. Most people where we live drink it all year long. "I really must go," I said, rising.

"We're not going to hear of it are we, Louella?" Preacher Dave lifted the basket at my feet. "You just rest a minute while I take this to the kitchen and Louella'll bring you a nice glass of tea—or there's coffee if you'd rather."

"Coffee would be fine," I said, trying to avoid what I knew would be Augusta's envious expression. I've stopped counting the number of cups she drinks in one day. But Augusta, apparently oblivious to our conversation, was examining a large framed photograph on the piano.

I looked about the room while waiting, and although some of the furnishings seemed worn, the oval hooked rug in colors of green and rose looked bright and new as did the coordinating swag over the front windows. A burgundy Christmas candle sat in a silk arrangement on a lovely mahogany side table. Grayson should be pleased to have such caring tenants.

I wandered over to look at the photograph that had captured Augusta's attention. It was a studio portrait of a pretty young woman, whose wide sweet smile made me want to smile, too. Her dark hair was cut in a becoming page boy and her large eyes held a spark of mischief.

"She's lovely," I said, noticing that Louella had come back into the room. "Is this your daughter?"

She nodded, setting my coffee cup aside. "Dinah. But she's gone now. Dead."

"Oh, I'm so sorry!" How horrible! *Why couldn't I keep my mouth shut? Having children myself, I could only imagine how tragic it would be to lose them.*

Louella moved quietly past me and came to stand by the piano. "This was hers, you know," she said, caressing the closed lid over the keyboard. "She did love to play."

I looked around to see Preacher Dave standing in the doorway. "Tell your cousin the vet thinks that little heifer we talked about is gonna be fine, and I mended that tear in the fence up there on the main road." And with that he turned and left the room.

I drank my coffee as quickly as I could, made my thanks, and left. Louella Tansey, looking frail and drab, a sad shadow of a woman, stood at the door gazing after me as if she wanted to follow.

FIVE

"DID YOU NOTICE PREACHER DAVE's face?" I said to Augusta as we drove away. "He was as white as Logan's cat."

Augusta immediately turned on the heater. "Logan's cat?"

"It's a term my grandmother used," I explained. "Except nobody seems to remember who Logan was."

"How sad for their daughter to die so young," she said. "I can see it's been a hardship for them."

"I wonder how she died, but I didn't dare ask. I could tell they didn't want to talk about it. As far as I know, nobody even knew they had a daughter."

I pulled up to the stop sign before entering the main road, and as I did, a pickup truck turned in and passed us going in the opposite direction. The young man behind the wheel had straw-colored hair pulled back in a ponytail and he made the turn so quickly he almost went into the ditch. I waved because that's what just about everybody does around here whether we know the driver or not, especially out in the country, but the driver didn't wave back.

Augusta turned to look over her shoulder. "Who was that?"

"I'm not sure but I think it might have been Jeremiah Tansey. Obviously in a hurry." In my rearview mirror I saw the faded blue truck disappearing in a cloud of dust.

As we passed the area behind the house at Willowbrook where we had found the tree I thought about stopping to get holly as we planned to decorate at Bellawood the next day, but it was already beginning to get dark and I didn't feel comfortable about going back there just yet—even with Augusta. Besides, there was always plenty of holly at Bellawood Plantation.

"I DO WISH WE HAD SOME HOLLY!" Genevieve Ellison said as she broke off a spray of pine. "This mantel just calls for it."

"I think they've used most of it in the other rooms," Nettie told her, "but we've plenty of cedar and spruce, and I think there's some hemlock down by the schoolhouse. That always looks graceful in an arrangement."

"I'll get it," I offered, glad of a chance to get some exercise. Several of us had congregated in the kitchen at Bellawood, which was separate from the main house, and a fire leapt on the great hearth blending the smell of wood smoke with that of the evergreens.

"'It's beginning to look a lot like Christmas!'" Idonia sang as she heaped pine cones into a large wooden bowl. Idonia's idea of decorating doesn't stray too far from Opal Henshaw's, but you can't go too far wrong with a bowl of pine cones. Idonia had been singing since she arrived that morning, and had even attempted (with a hilarious jumbling of lyrics) "The Twelve Days of Christmas."

Melrose, she told us, had given her his Christmas present early: an antique gold locket in the shape of a dogwood blossom with tiny seed pearls in the center, and it dangled now against her forest green sweater. The locket had once belonged to Melrose's grandmother, she explained earlier, and she had hesitated about accepting anything so personal, but Melrose had insisted.

"It doesn't do a thing for me," he'd told her, laughing. "Who else is going to wear it?"

Idonia fingered it lovingly as she paused to admire her work. "Melrose said it had six pearls in it originally," she said, "but two of them are missing. Sometime after the holidays he's going to see if he can get them replaced for me." And with that remark she drifted into "Jingle Bells" and began to poke cedar boughs into a ceramic jar. The small room had become increasingly warm with the wood fire and I was glad I'd elected to wear a cotton shirt and jeans as had most of the others. Idonia must have been uncomfortable in her sweater as I noticed she stayed as far away from the fireplace as possible.

"Why don't some of you help me make a swag for the front doorway?" Genevieve asked with a critical eye on Idonia's attempts at arranging. "We can cut the greenery in lengths and spread them out here on the table to wire together."

I knew from experience that sounded easier than it actually was, so I put on my jacket and went outside for the hemlock. When I returned with the greenery, Nettie trailed it along the big pine mantel and tucked it behind fat red candles along with clusters of red nandina berries. Idonia, I noticed, was still attempting to make a swag while Genevieve worked quietly behind her repairing the damage. Still humming, Idonia apparently hadn't noticed, or if she had, she didn't care. I hoped this wasn't too good to last.

We spent the rest of our time at Bellawood in the main house, tucking sprigs of spruce and pine behind picture frames, putting candles in every room, and setting out bowls of nuts and apples. Someone with more artistic ability than I had made a feathery wreath of evergreens interspersed with fluffy white bolls of cotton for the front door. It reminded me of the wreath on the door of the Green Cottage back at Willowbrook, and for a while that put a bit of a damper on my Christmas spirit.

I told Nettie about my visit to the Tanseys on the drive home together. (Idonia was entertaining Melrose for dinner and had to stop for groceries.)

"Did you know they had a daughter who died?" I asked.

"No, but then I don't know them very well," Nettie said. "From all I've heard Preacher Dave seems to be a hard worker and everyone says he's doing a good job filling in at the church for Luther. I've only seen his wife once or twice—shy little creature."

"I think they go to Chandler's Creek Baptist Church out on Sawmill Road," I said. "Preacher Dave's a part-time minister there."

"Wonder where they lived before they came here?" Nettie said. "Nobody seems to know much about them."

"Maybe they're just trying to escape sad memories."

"Well, they'd better brace up because it doesn't look like they're going to escape Opal Henshaw and her fruitcake," Nettie said. "Reckon Claudia will work up enough gumption to tell her she's not going to help with the 'run'?"

I laughed. "I doubt it. Let's just hope nobody offers us any while we're caroling this weekend."

"I CAN'T WAIT TO MEET Idonia's admirer," I said to Augusta that night after supper. "But I'm not quite sure what to think. She's known this Melrose about a month yet he's given her a locket he says belonged to his grandmother. Wouldn't you think a family heirloom like that would go to one of his children?"

"Maybe he doesn't have any children," Augusta said. With a smile she added a tiny gilded angel to an arrangement of hemlock and pine and stepped back to examine it. The caroling party was days away and the only Christmas decoration I'd put up was an evergreen wreath on the front door. Now the two of us were doing our best to make the house look festive with the leftover greenery I'd brought from Bellawood.

"If he has any, Idonia hasn't mentioned it," I said. "Ellis said he works part time for his cousin at the funeral home, but surely he didn't come to Stone's Throw just for that." I rummaged in the box of decorations until I found the stuffed reindeer with a bell around its neck that always spent the season on Julie's bed and set it aside. "I wonder what did bring him here?"

"Perhaps we'll know in time, but from what you tell me, your friend seems happy with things as they are, so it would seem advisable to let sleeping cats be," she said, refilling her coffee mug. Augusta rarely sips coffee; she *drinks* it, and she did that now. So fortified, she set the mug aside and with flying fingers went about weaving the remaining greenery into a fragrant swag. My giggle at her jumbled expression seemed to escape her completely.

"That's just the point," I explained. "Idonia's marriage wasn't very happy—only lasted a few years until her husband found somebody else and left her to raise their little boy alone. I don't think Idonia has ever gotten over the hurt, and I hate to think of it happening again."

The stones shimmered green and gold as Augusta twined her long necklace through her fingers. "Your friend is a grown woman, Lucy Nan, and she makes choices just as most people do. I'm sure you'll agree it's best to let her make her own decisions…"

I followed her as she carried the swag down the hall to the living room where she draped it over the mantel. It looked fantastic. "Everybody will think I hired a decorator," I told her.

"…still," Augusta continued, "I don't believe it would be inappropriate if we looked into this fellow's background—inconspicuously, of course."

"Fine," I said. "He'll be coming here for the caroling party, and Augusta, I don't know of anyone who can be more inconspicuous than you! We'll have to do a rush job of decorating the tree before the party," I said as I swept clippings from under the kitchen table. "Ben and I are going out to Willowbrook tomorrow to cut one so I guess I'd better get the decorations down from the attic."

"What did your policeman friend think about the possibility of a hidden staircase?" she asked.

"Not much. He said they looked around inside to see if they could find where one might be but didn't have any luck." I shrugged. "There's probably nothing to it. Mimmer always did have a good imagination. She said all the Vances do."

"Oh, my goodness, that reminds me!" Augusta let the dustpan clatter to the floor. "I forgot all about the phone call. I don't suppose you've checked your messages."

I shook my head. "Hadn't had a chance. What phone call?"

"Your cousin Grayson called while you were out. It seems his grandson Vance and his young lady would like to see the old home place and asked if you might meet them there tomorrow. I believe he's expecting you to return his call."

I looked at the clock. It was a few minutes after nine. I hoped my cousin hadn't already gone to bed.

But he sounded wide awake when I reached him.

"My friend Ben Maxwell and I plan to go out to Willowbrook to get my tree in the morning—probably sometime after ten," I told him. "Would that be too early for Vance and Jamie to meet us there?"

"Should be fine," he said. "I gave them a key to the house, but they don't know Dave Tansey and he doesn't know them. Didn't want him to think they had a prowler about—especially after what happened last week."

"Good thinking," I said. "I'll phone Preacher Dave in the morning so they'll know what we plan to do."

"They never did find out what that fellow was about, did they?" Grayson asked. "Was there no kind of identification or any kind of transportation?"

"Not that I know of," I said. "The police seem to think he was probably a vagrant taking shelter there for the night—of course, there are things they don't tell me."

BEN SHOWED UP the next morning in time for coffee and some of Augusta's pumpkin bread before leaving for Willowbrook. Augusta won't admit it, but I think she has kind of a crush on Ben Maxwell. I noticed the bread was fresh-from-the-oven warm and the coffee strong and steaming hot just as he likes it. They've never met, of course.

"It's going to be weird going back to Willowbrook," I said

as we got ready to leave. "I don't think I'll ever feel the same way about it again."

Ben kissed the top of my head as he helped me with my jacket. "You don't sound like you have much confidence in my ability to protect you. I'm crushed."

I gave him a quick kiss, then shoved him out the door before he got a notion to linger. Clementine, of course, wanted to go along, too, and jumped into the front seat between us. "I know exactly where the tree is so it shouldn't take too long to find it, but my cousin Vance and his girlfriend are supposed to meet us out there to see the house," I told him. "Nellie Virginia— that's Vance's mother—thinks he might have an idea of living at Willowbrook someday." I reached over the dog to touch his hand. "I hope you're not in a hurry."

"My time is yours," he said, giving my fingers a squeeze. "I'm not working on anything that can't wait."

Ben is a talented furniture craftsman who does a lot of work restoring antiques at Bellawood, which is where we became friends. His reddish brown hair and beard, now streaked with gray, are an indication of his Scottish heritage, and his blue eyes have the intensity to warm you through and through or pierce you with an icy glance, depending on the situation. I don't even like to think about how dull my life had become before Ben Maxwell ordered me out of his workshop at Bellawood along with the children in my grandson Teddy's kindergarten class. That was over a year ago and to tell the truth it could have been a disaster as a number of yelling children pursued several yelping puppies through his sacred domain, tracking sawdust, scattering nails, and upsetting tools along the way. Ben, I thought at the time, had been unnecessarily gruff. Now he and Teddy have become great friends—and he has a special place in my life as well.

Once at Willowbrook it didn't take long to locate the tree and Ben quickly sawed it down and carried it back to the van. The weather, although brisk, wasn't as cold as it had been the week before and while Ben trimmed the base of the tree and lifted it into the back of his vehicle I shed my heavy jacket to race with Clementine in and out among the evergreens while we waited for the others to arrive. It was almost eleven when I saw the approaching car.

"We were about to give up on you," I called as Vance and Jamie pulled up in front of the house.

My young cousin gave me a hug as we made introductions. "Sorry to keep you waiting," he said, "but I decided to drop by the Green Cottage first just to let the Tanseys know who we are." He smiled at Jamie. "Didn't want to get shot!"

"Did you see Preacher Dave?" I asked.

He shook his head. "Nope. Only his wife—Louella, isn't it? She was just leaving for work."

"Said her husband had already left for the church and their son works somewhere in Rock Hill," Jamie added.

"Right. When I phoned out there earlier this morning, Louella said they would probably all be gone. Works at that fabric shop on the other side of town."

Vance felt in his pocket for the key to the house. "Anybody ready for a tour? I haven't been inside since I was little but I re-member thinking how beautiful it was. I'm curious to see it again."

"I hope you won't be disappointed," I said, knowing that time and neglect hadn't been kind to the old family home.

"I can hardly wait!" Jamie started walking a little ahead of the rest of us but she stopped suddenly and stood looking at the house. "Is somebody supposed to be in there?" she asked.

"Not that I know of," I said. "Why?"

Jamie pointed to an upstairs window. "I thought I saw someone up there. Looked like a woman. Didn't any of you see her?"

Vance frowned. "There shouldn't be anyone in there. Are you sure you saw somebody?"

Jamie hesitated before speaking. "I thought I did…I could

swear it moved, but I guess it could have been a curtain or something."

I didn't want to tell her there weren't any curtains in the house. "Must've been poor Celia," I said and told her about the family ghost.

"Ghost or not, I think we should check this out," Vance said, turning to Ben. "What do you say we take a look inside? If there's anyone in there I'd like to know who they are and what they're doing here."

"Oh no, you don't!" I told him. "You're not leaving me out here. If you two go inside, I'm going, too."

Jamie nodded. "Count me in, too," she said.

I slipped back into my jacket as we huddled on the portico waiting for Vance to unlock the heavy front door. And that was when we heard it. Someone was playing a violin and the music was coming from inside the house.

Suddenly it seemed to have turned much colder.

SIX

"THIS IS RIDICULOUS!" Ben said, wiping his feet before entering—as if a few extra clumps of dirt would matter to years' accumulation of dust. "There has to be a rational explanation for this."

Vance, who walked ahead of us, stopped so short I almost collided with him. "Can you hear anything now? It seems to be over," he said, putting out a hand to quiet us.

Standing there in a silent knot, we waited until my feet grew numb and I just had to shuffle a bit. "I think the concert's finished," I told them.

"Well, I'm going in search of the soloist," Ben said, striding into what had once been my grandmother's dining room. Vance chose to go in the other direction and began poking behind doors and into crannies in the drawing room leaving Jamie and me alone in the vast entrance hall, where even our whispers echoed around us. Clementine, who had chosen to chase a rabbit rather than accompany us inside the house, was of little or no use to us here.

"Kids!" Jamie said finally. "Has to be some kind of prank."

"Most likely," I said, hoping it was true. I didn't tell her that Ellis had heard similar music the morning we discovered the body beneath the balcony, and even Augusta had admitted to hearing a scuttling noise. Doors opened and closed and drawers slammed shut as the two men explored the rooms beyond, which included a large kitchen, small parlor, and two adjoining bedrooms in the back. Willowbrook was a solid square house built to last through the years, which it obviously had. The four rooms in the front shared two chimneys while the larger of the bedrooms in the back, the one that had been my grandmother's, had its own fireplace. The smaller room adjoining it had none.

Jamie and I wandered into the drawing room, which seemed to be the sunnier, and therefore the warmer of the rooms to wait while Ben and Vance stormed about like a dedicated SWAT team thumping and bumping about. "Don't worry," I told her, "I'm sure they'll be all right." She couldn't see that I had a death grip on the cell phone in my jacket pocket.

She managed a smile. "Vance has told me so much about this old place, I just had to see it—didn't expect such an adventure! It is beautiful, though—or it could be. I can see why he cares so much about it."

And I hope you care about him if you're planning to live here, I thought, sidestepping a pile of debris. The house smelled of mice and mildew.

"Come look at this." Vance appeared in the doorway and led us into the larger of the bedrooms. "Somebody has been using this fireplace." He kicked aside a couple of empty food cans and a crumpled bread wrapper. "It's a wonder this whole place hasn't burned to the ground."

We found the charred remains of a fire in the grate and a few pieces of firewood were stacked on the hearth along with an empty half pint of some kind of liquor I'd never heard of.

"Trespassers are getting in somehow," Ben offered. "Looks like you're going to have to start boarding the place up."

"I'll ask Granddad to speak to Mr. Tansey. I'm sure he makes an effort, but just locking the doors doesn't seem to be working." Hands on his hips, Vance stared at the clutter around the fireplace. "We can't have this kind of thing!"

"Preacher Dave says he's run off squatters from time to time, and I know he tries to keep an eye on the place, but with his other duties, I guess he can't check on things like he should." I found that I had trouble speaking through the knot in my throat. I was glad my grandmother couldn't see her precious Willowbrook now.

We went upstairs in single file to find a similar jumble of litter. The fireplaces had been sealed off in two of the four bedrooms but a pigeon, which had apparently flown in through a broken window, lay dead in a corner of one, and a dirty, tattered sleeping bag had been tossed in another. I wondered if it had belonged to the man who plunged from the balcony. Mouse droppings were evident everywhere and I glanced at Jamie to see how she was reacting to her tour of her boyfriend's ancestral home. Noticing the attention, she merely shrugged. "I think you might want to invent a better mousetrap," she told him.

Ben seemed to be taking careful note of the walls, paying particular attention to areas around the fireplaces. In one of the front bedrooms, cabinets had been built on either side of the fireplace and he meticulously investigated both of them, tapping from every angle.

"Maybe there's a lever somewhere that makes it revolve," I teased. "That's the way it works in the movies."

"I did think we might find a tape recorder or something like that," Ben said, running his fingers along the sides of the cabinets. "That music had to come from somewhere."

Vance stood at one of the two long windows that faced the front. A shutter hung crazily to one side and pale winter sunlight cut a crooked pathway across the grimy floor. "There's a drainpipe loose out here," he said, "and the wind *was* blowing earlier. Do you think that might have been what we heard?"

"If it was, it was playing a tune!" Jamie told him. "And I think I've heard that song before."

It had sounded familiar to me, too, I said. "Did you recognize what it was?"

Jamie shook her head. "No, but I'm sure it didn't come from any drainpipe!"

I repeated the snatch of music in my head. The notes were

from a few bars of a longer composition, and I knew they would haunt me until I learned what it was. During the drive home I hummed them aloud so I wouldn't forget, and Ben agreed that what we had heard at Willowbrook had been deliberately played for our benefit.

We had found nothing in any of the bedrooms upstairs or in the large room behind them that ran across the back of the house. Mimmer had told me that at various times that room had been a ballroom, a schoolroom, even quarters for a bachelor uncle, and later a storeroom for the family's discards. When we emptied the house after Mimmer died I rescued a perfectly beautiful Windsor chair that now sits in the corner of my living room from what my grandmother referred to as "the junk room."

"I hope Vance and his family won't waste any time closing up that house," Ben said as we waited at a traffic light. "The kids around here have obviously heard rumors of your family ghost, and some have even claimed they saw a woman in a hoopskirt on the balcony. That poor fellow's death out there just added fuel to the fire." He reached over to nuzzle Clementine's ears as she once again snuggled between us. "If anyone is injured in a fire out there—God forbid—your cousin Grayson would be held responsible."

"And I doubt if he even has insurance," I admitted. "It's almost impossible to get a policy on an empty house." Although I knew from my grandson that local students were out of school for a teachers' workday, I really didn't believe our mysterious violinist was part of a harmless prank. After all, Augusta herself had said we hadn't seen the end of the trouble at Willowbrook. And Augusta was usually right.

BEN HAD A MEETING about an order for a cherry writing desk with somebody in Columbia that afternoon, but he took time to help me get the tree in a stand and put it in my living-room window before leaving. Later that evening my son, Roger, and his wife, Jessica, would drop by with Teddy to help me decorate. Meanwhile, Augusta got us started by stringing the lights and the delicate garlands that looked like miniature red apples. Charlie had brought them to me from a business trip several years before, and for a while after his death I couldn't bring myself to put them on the tree.

"I believe it's almost as pretty as the one we got for the church," I said as Augusta swirled strings of tiny white lights in a perfect pattern. I told her about the music we had heard that morning but didn't try to repeat the tune. Augusta loves to sing but her notes don't always ring true, and I knew it would be a waste of time to ask her if she knew it. Why, she told me herself she had never even been allowed to audition for the heavenly choir.

Now she stepped back to appraise what she had done, and apparently satisfied, sank onto the rose brocade rocking chair by the fireplace. I seldom keep a fire in there as we usually spent our time in the small sitting room, but since the family was coming tonight, Augusta had agreed to build one, and now a happy little blaze crackled in the grate.

"Did you ever find the source of that music?" she asked, trying to avoid rocking on Clementine's tail.

"No such luck, and believe me, we looked that whole place over, room by room. Ben took a lot of time checking those cabinets on either side of the fireplace, too, but he couldn't find anywhere that might be a hiding place."

"I don't suppose you heard anything else?" Augusta fingered her dazzling necklace, flashing gold and amber in the fire's light.

"You mean like the scuttling sound you heard?" I said. "No, but there must've been an army of mice in there! The whole place is a mess! Mimmer would just be sick if she knew."

"Well, she doesn't know, so don't worry on her account, but it is a shame to see a fine old home go to ruin." Augusta rose to check the macaroni and cheese she had made for supper and I followed to pop some corn for the tree. I'm hard put to come up with something to serve my daughter-in-law, Jessica, since she's a vegetarian and won't even indulge in an innocent hamburger now and then. Thank goodness she isn't one of those people who won't eat any animal products or I'd really be in a bind.

Corn popped in the microwave while Augusta sprinkled nutmeg over a bowl of homemade applesauce and I put together ingredients for a green salad. Supper was ready to serve and the two of us already had a good start on stringing the popcorn when Teddy burst in the back door and threw himself down to wallow with Clementine on the kitchen rug. Augusta, as usual, disappeared from view.

"Give Clementine a hug and then hurry and wash your hands. Supper's ready," I told him, knowing his mother would probably haul out the antiseptic wipes if she saw the dog licking Teddy in the face. Jessica has become adjusted to having Clementine around, but she's still having a problem with doggy hair, doggy slobber, and what she imagines to be doggy germs.

Roger waited until Teddy and his mother were stringing popcorn for the tree after supper before bringing up the subject of the unfortunate incident at Willowbrook. Augusta and I had been baking that week and now he snatched a Santa-shaped cookie and bit off its head as I arranged them on a platter. Jessica doesn't serve sweets in their home but I think she's finally given up on mine.

"So, Mom," he began, reaching for another, "you seem to be starting off the holly-jolly season with a bang—or should I say, a thud? Have you developed some kind of sinister detector that leads you to dead bodies? I'm beginning to wonder if it's safe for you to be about! Should we hire a bodyguard?"

Now, I'm proud of my son and love him all to pieces, but since he's been made chair of the History Department at Sarah Bedford, our local college, he's gotten obnoxiously bossy. I chose that moment to tell him so. "Look," I said, "the man was already dead when we found him. I doubt very much if he picked that morning to jump or fall or whatever from the balcony just because I was in the vicinity." (I didn't dare mention the notion that he might have been pushed!)

"Well, something's going on out there, and I hope you and Aunt Ellis will have the good sense to stay out of it. Let Cousin Grayson worry about it. After all, it's his house." Roger stood to clear the table while I scraped dishes at the sink. Ellis is the closest thing to an aunt my two will ever have since neither Charlie nor I had any sisters and my brother can't seem to stay married. "Preacher Dave seems to think the guy might've been a homeless person who probably had too much to drink," he said, stacking glasses on top of plates until they leaned precariously, "and I can't get a word out of Ed down at the Police Department."

Ed Tillman and Roger had been friends since kindergarten and I knew him well enough to know he could clam up tighter than a miser's purse. I wasn't having any better luck with my friend Kemper Mungo.

"Maybe he doesn't have anything to tell," I said, rescuing the tottering stack, "but if I learn anything, I promise I'll let you know."

"Just promise you'll stay away from there." He brushed my cheek with a kiss. "I worry about you, you know."

"I know," I said, giving his arm a damp pat. There was no way I was going to tell him about our experiences at Willowbrook that morning. I just hoped I could count on Ben to keep his mouth shut, too.

"I RAN INTO NETTIE at the library this morning and she told me you had made new window treatments for Julie's room," Jessica mentioned later as we finished decorating the tree. "When do I get to see them?"

"Anytime," I said, watching Roger boost Teddy up to put the star on top of the tree. It was a pitiful-looking star my great-grandmother had made by sewing gold oiled paper to cardboard but, dog-eared as it was, it was tradition, and traditions die hard in our family.

"What about now?" Jessica was already on her way upstairs so there was nothing I could do but follow.

Augusta had fashioned simple tab curtains from a heavy cotton blend, and since Julie loved purple, the pattern featured inch-wide vertical stripes in that color against a white background. At intervals, a scattering of fern fronds lent a bright touch of green.

Jessica fingered the fabric and inspected the lining. Naturally, she found it perfect. "This is absolutely lovely!" she exclaimed, turning to me with a new glow of respect. I know she must have been wondering how I learned to sew so well after the disaster of Teddy's Halloween costume—or what was meant to be Teddy's Halloween costume—but, of course, she was too polite to mention it. "I've been looking for something similar for that little upstairs bedroom. Bought those curtains in a hurry when we first moved in, and I never have liked them. Did it take you very long to make these?"

"Oh, not too long…I worked on them off and on, of course." I stiffened. I could *feel* Augusta standing behind me and I didn't dare turn around.

"Do you think you might show me how? I hate to pay somebody to make them, and I'd really like to learn if you think it wouldn't be too terribly hard." Jessica turned imploring blue eyes on me and I felt like the lowest kind of worm. My daughter-in-law seldom asks favors and I really wanted to do something special to please her.

"Great jumpin' Jehoshaphat! Don't tell me you *made* those!" Roger stood in the doorway, his eyes wide with shock—an expression, I thought, which was unnecessarily exaggerated. "When did you learn to *sew*?"

"I'm afraid I'm not a very good instructor, but if you'll measure your windows and decide on the fabric, I'll be happy to make your curtains," I said, turning to his wife.

Behind him in the hallway Augusta laughed silently.

"I GUESS I STEPPED INTO it this time," I told her after the others had left. "You are going to help me, aren't you?"

"Of course, but they really aren't all that difficult to make," she said. "I could show you how."

"When I was in high school, I made a C-minus in home economics—and I was lucky to get it," I said. "Our teacher, Mrs. Settlemyer, retired after that year. Everybody said she went to live in Alabama with her daughter but we always suspected the poor soul had a nervous breakdown…. You might be an angel," I told her, "but you're not a saint!"

The two of us sat in the darkened living room watching the lights of the tree reflected in the window while the fire burned low on the hearth. Since Teddy had done most of the decorating, a lot of the ornaments hung on the lower branches but that was fine with me. I closed my eyes, drinking in the fresh cedar smell. "Just two more days until the caroling party," I reminded Augusta, "and we'll finally get to meet Melrose DuBois!"

SEVEN

THE NEXT DAY WAS FRIDAY and Weigelia Jones was coming to
help me get ready for The Thursdays' caroling party the following night. Weigelia and I became friends when I was her tutor
in the literacy program several years earlier, and when I'm in
a bind she's good enough to work me in on her house-cleaning
schedule. There's no spot of dirt that can elude Weigelia Jones's
keen eyes, no cobweb too far from her reach, and when I see
her coming I want to throw my arms around her and shout hal-
lelujah. Instead, I put on a huge pot of coffee. Weigelia loves
it almost as much as Augusta, only she fills her cup about
halfway with cream.

I was hurrying through my breakfast of cereal and orange
juice that morning when it occurred to me that Augusta was
trying to get my attention. "Did you say something?" I asked,
rinsing my bowl at the sink. I didn't want to be in Weigelia's
way when she started working her miracles on my kitchen
floor.

"Only two or three times," Augusta said. "You must have
been a million miles away. Is something on your mind?"

"It's that blasted song!" I admitted. "That little snatch of
melody we heard at Willowbrook yesterday. I can't get it out
of my head and it's about to drive me crazy."

"The violin music?" Augusta tapped her slender fingers on
the table. "Why don't you ask someone who might be familiar
with the piece—perhaps someone at the college. Didn't you
tell me there was a group who played—"

"The Fiddlesticks! Of course! Our postmaster, Albert Grady,
plays the violin and so does his wife, Miranda. I have to buy

Christmas stamps anyway, and today would be as good a time as any." And I bent to kiss her angelic cheek. "Augusta, you're a genius! Now, what was it you wanted to say?"

Augusta flushed, which meant she was pleased. Although she tells me vanity is folly, I've seen her admire her own reflection too many times to take her seriously. "I asked what you had in mind to serve for your caroling party tomorrow," she said. "I saw a recipe for individual meat pies in the newspaper the other day, and—"

"Perfect!" I said. "We'll probably be chilled when we return so I thought I'd have some kind of hot soup…"

"Hmm…that butternut squash soup would be good…with a bit of ginger and nutmeg and a dash of sherry, of course. We had it last Christmas, remember?"

"Good but troublesome. Too much stewing and brewing!" I told her.

"I don't mind stewing and brewing," she said in what I thought was just a hint of self-righteousness. (I didn't say so, of course.)

And so we decided on the menu—or Augusta decided on it.

Not that I minded one bit. "Naturally, The Thursdays will bring finger foods," I said. And I could guess what most of them would be. Ellis would bring a chafing dish with her famous hot clam dip; Jo Nell, sweet-and-sour meatballs; Zee, chicken salad puffs; Claudia usually brought marinated mushrooms; Nettie made a wonderful cheese ball; and I could count on Idonia to furnish fresh fruit.

"Of course, we'll have sweets coming out of our ears," I said, thinking of all the Christmas cakes and cookies everyone would bring.

Augusta's eyes grew wide. "Out of your *ears*?" she gasped, and I laughed so, I hardly had breath to explain that it was merely an expression.

I was still laughing when I heard Weigelia's car pull up

behind the house. Besides going to the post office, I had several other errands to run and I asked Augusta if she'd like to go with me as she usually preferred to be out of the house while Weigelia cleaned. "Sometimes I have a feeling she suspects I'm here," she once told me, "and I don't like to take any chances."

But this time she had other plans. "Ellis has decided she wants plum pudding for Christmas dinner," she explained, "and I promised to help her make it. If you're going by the library, however, I'm almost out of something to read." Augusta has been on a mystery kick for the past few months and has already worked her way to the M–P section in the Stone's Throw Library. I promised to see what I could do.

WEIGELIA HADN'T EVEN finished her first cup of coffee before I realized she knew something I didn't. She hadn't had much to say when she came in lugging that big old bucket with all the brushes and soaps she likes to use. (She turns up her nose at mine.) Today she wore the new Reeboks her sister Celeste gave her for her birthday and a long purple skirt that touched the top of her rolled-down socks. The "ten-gallon" red plastic handbag she carries had been duly deposited behind the pantry door along with her faithful green plaid coat.

"Okay," I said. "What is it?"

"I guess you want me to do Julie's room since she be comin' for Christmas," she said, pouring a second cup to go with her muffin.

"You might run the sweeper in there and flip the dust around a little." I sat across from her and stared until she had to look at me. She hates it when I do that. "It's something about that man who died out at Willowbrook, isn't it? You've been talking to Kemper, haven't you?"

Weigelia's cousin Kemper Mungo is a sergeant with the Stone's Throw police and if anybody could worm information from him, it would be Weigelia Jones. Now it was up to me to get her to turn loose and tell.

It wasn't easy. "You know Kemper ain't supposed to be talking to me 'bout things like that—and he sure don't want me spreadin' it around," she informed me.

"And *you* know I'll find out eventually. Besides, *The Messenger* is going to get wind of it sooner or later." *The Messenger* is Stone's Throw's weekly newspaper, and when its editor, Josie Kiker, gets the scent of a story, she's like a hungry dog going after a bone. "After all," I reminded her, "Ellis and I did find the body. That should entitle us to something."

Weigelia finished her coffee, and in slow motion, rose, rinsed her cup, and put it in the dishwasher. "They found out that man's name," she said finally.

"The dead man? Who was he?"

She tied an apron around her middle and took her sweet time about doing it. "Last name Clark, I think…wait just a minute… I wrote it down."

I waited while Weigelia reached into her vast bosom for a scrap of paper and handed it to me. And then she laughed. *She* knew that I knew she was eventually going to tell me. The name *Dexter Clark* was printed in block letters on what had been the flap of an envelope. "Who's this Dexter Clark when he's at home?" she said.

I shrugged. "Beats me."

"Kemper say he got a record: breaking and entering, drunk and disorderly—you name it." She shook her head. "Not a very nice man."

"Not nice at all," I said, "but that kind of explains what he was doing at Willowbrook."

Weigelia grabbed her polish and dust rag and headed for the living room. "What you mean?" she asked, pausing in the doorway.

"Breaking and entering, and being drunk and disorderly," I explained.

According to Weigelia, the dead man didn't have a permanent address so nobody seemed to know where he came from or what he was doing here—other than taking shelter. And if my cousin Grayson didn't do something about securing Willowbrook, I was afraid he wouldn't be the last casualty there.

THE LINES IN THE POST OFFICE reached to the door and I waved to Clarence Allen, one of the clerks, who waited patiently on a customer. He nodded in return, eyes glazed. It was mid-December and people were still mailing packages. The postmaster's door was closed and I knocked softly and called out to Albert. The Gradys are members of our church and I've always found him to be pleasant and even-tempered. However, as I said, it *was* the middle of December.

He looked up from his computer, glasses halfway down his nose. "Lucy Nan! How can I help you?" I noticed he didn't ask me to sit.

"I realize this is a bad time," I began, "but this tune is driving me crazy and I thought you might recognize it." I told him about the mysterious melody we'd heard at Willowbrook and even went so far as to hum a few bars.

His expression was blank. "Well, it does sound familiar, but I have no idea what it is. I hope you've told the police about this, Lucy Nan. It all sounds peculiar to me, especially after that fellow was found dead out there."

"My cousin thinks it's probably a prank, but I thought if I could just find out the name of the song it might have something to do with what's going on out there," I told him.

Albert pushed up his glasses and sighed. "If anybody might be able to tell you it would be Miranda. She has perfect pitch, you know—never forgets a melody—although to tell you the truth, I think you ought to leave it to the police."

"She still teaching at the middle school?"

He glanced at the clock. "Yes, but she has a free period in about an hour. Why don't you drop by and ask her? She'll probably be glad of a break."

I thanked him, stood in line for my stamps, and phoned the

school to let Miranda know I was coming. By the time I collected Augusta's books at the library, I had five minutes to get to there.

Miranda is choral director at the school and I found her in the music room surrounded by stacks and stacks of sheet music. "We're as ready as we're going to be for our holiday concert tomorrow night," she said when I came in. "Now, I have to decide what we need to work on for the spring!"

"Albert said you never forget a song and might be able to identify something for me," I said, explaining the reason for my visit.

"Why don't you hum a few bars and we'll give it a try," she said, sitting at the piano.

When I finished, she repeated the notes on the piano, adding even more of the melody. "That's it!" I said. "Please tell me you know what it is!"

Miranda laughed. "Of course. It's Romanian Rhapsody no. 1 by George Enescu. I played it in a concert once when I was in college. Beautiful piece."

I nodded. "It has a haunting quality, don't you think? Maybe that's why whoever's doing this chose that particular song." I told her the story about the family ghost and how some have even claimed to see a figure in a period gown.

She frowned. "And this was supposed to have happened when?"

"Sometime during the War Between the States," I said. "Probably around 1863."

"Then they need to go back and do their homework," Miranda said. "Enescu wasn't born for more than a decade after that!

"I don't want to scare you, Lucy Nan," she added, "but it sounds as if somebody might be trying to frighten people away. They could easily use a CD or a tape of the music to give the ghostly effect—but why? What's going on out there they don't want anyone to know about?"

I had been thinking the same thing, and the more I thought about it, the madder I got. In fact, I was practically seething by the time I pulled up behind the Stone's Throw Police Department. The grocery store could wait!

Weigelia's cousin Kemper wasn't in but I was lucky enough to catch Captain Alonzo Hardy in an idle moment, and by the time he saw me coming, it was too late to run and hide.

"I want to know what's going on at Willowbrook," I demanded, telling him of our experience the day before. "First, a man is killed out there, and now this! Are you sure you searched that place thoroughly? And just who was the man we found?" I didn't want to get Kemper in trouble by admitting I already knew the dead man's name.

He sighed and motioned for me to sit, then proceeded to tell me what I already knew. "I've spoken with Dave Tansey and he's promised to board up the more accessible windows and do more to discourage vagrants out there. That old house is practically an open invitation to trespassers, I'm afraid. As far as we could tell, this man who was killed hadn't been drinking—fellow by the name of Dexter Clark. Had a record, though—petty stuff mostly. Didn't seem to have a permanent address." The captain picked up a pencil and rolled it between his palms. "No tellin' how long he'd been camping there. Reckon he knew a good thing when he saw it, and others, no doubt, have followed suit."

"But the music—"

"Shoot, everybody around here knows that crazy old ghost tale! Somebody rigged that up to scare people away." He tossed the pencil aside. "I'm telling you, we looked over every inch of that place, checked very nook and cranny where they might hide something like that, and came up with zilch!"

I told him Ben and Vance hadn't had any better luck.

"Well, we'll try to give it another look-see. Maybe we can surprise them, find out what this is all about…could be just some kids with nothing better to do, but if you'll take my advice, Ms. Pilgrim, you'll stay away from there."

I TOLD AUGUSTA ABOUT our conversation that night as I helped her make the small meat pies for the party. I browned the ground beef and combined it with onion, spices, and other ingredients while Augusta made the pastry and cut circles for the pies. She planned to make the soup the next morning, she said, and we had decided to serve hot spiced punch when everyone returned from caroling.

"You mentioned that Louella Tansey was at home when your cousin arrived yesterday," she reminded me. "Do you think it might have been her?"

"I don't see how she could have gotten to the house before Vance and Jamie. They hadn't been there more than a minute or so before we heard the violin. Besides, I'm sure we would've seen her. And she said Jeremiah had already left for work."

Augusta's hands flew as she spooned filling onto circles of pastry, folded them over, and crimped the edges. In what seemed only seconds, neat rows of pies lined the baking sheets ready to pop into the oven. I watched in silent amazement as she whisked an egg together with a spoonful of water for the glaze. "Once this party is behind us, perhaps I can do a bit of investigating on my own," she said, sliding the pastries into the refrigerator to be baked at the last minute.

"We really won't have that much to do tomorrow," I said. As usual, Weigelia had left the house spotless.

"What carols do you plan to sing?" Augusta gave her Christmas apron a jaunty flip and hung it in the pantry. She had made one for both of us, and hers was a patchwork creation of stars and bells in silver, lavender, and blue, while mine featured a similar pattern in red, green, and gold.

It would have been hard not to notice the wistfulness in her voice. "Oh, the usual songs, I guess. Why don't *you* come, Augusta?"

"Do you think I might?" I am not exaggerating when I say her smile was radiant. "I wouldn't sing, of course."

"Of course you might! It'll be fun! Weigelia's coming, too." Weigelia had offered to help with refreshments the next night, but I persuaded her we'd much rather have her company and her voice. Weigelia has this deep, rich contralto that sounds like the soul of an angel is breaking free from somewhere deep inside her. I guess it's kind of like Augusta should sound, if only she could.

EIGHT

"ARE THEY HERE YET?" Ellis whispered, standing in the doorway.

"Not yet! Hurry and come inside—it's freezing out there!" I knew who she meant without asking, as I was just as eager as she was to get a look at Idonia's mysterious Melrose DuBois.

Ellis's husband Bennett crowded in after her, beating his gloved hands together. "You picked a dandy night for caroling. Must be twenty degrees out there!"

"Actually, it's twenty-six," I informed him. "Ben has a bar set up in the kitchen if you need some antifreeze."

"Everybody else is here," I told Ellis. She had brought her clam dip over earlier and now hurried into the dining room to adjust the heat under the chafing dish. Claudia's husband Brian hovered over the table competing with Zee for the sweet-and-sour meat-balls, while Jo Nell's Paul kept Ben company in the kitchen. Bennett, I noticed, soon joined them.

Nettie, who stood at the living room window nursing a glass of red wine, held aside the curtain to peer into the street. "Seems they should be here by now…you don't suppose she's forgotten the time?"

"Oh, dear! What if they don't come?" Jo Nell looked over Nettie's shoulder. "Do you think something's happened?"

"*I think* I'm going to have some of these appetizers everybody's wolfing down with a nice glass of wine," Ellis said, warming herself by the fire.

"Sounds like a plan to me." Weigelia set a dish of mixed nuts on the coffee table and stretched out her hands to the blaze. "Only I'm gonna warm my insides with some good hot coffee before I go out in the cold." She shook her head. "I think the whole lot of us are crazy—that's what I think!"

Weigelia has cleaned for most of The Thursdays at one time or another, and not only knows about the dust balls under the sofa, but our other secrets as well. Ellis finally admitted to me that she'd given Weigelia her grandmother's treasured recipe for frozen fruit salad years before she gave it to me.

Claudia moved among us, a glass of wine in one hand and a tray of her marinated mushrooms in the other. "Well, I wish they'd hurry and get here before I lose my nerve to go out and face the elements. I don't know how I'll manage to sing if my teeth are chattering!"

"Have another glass of wine," Zee advised her, lifting her own.

"Has anybody ever *seen* Melrose?" Jo Nell asked. "I wonder what he looks like."

Nettie turned from her vigil by the window. "You'll soon find out—they just drove up!"

"Everybody hush, now! Just act natural," Zee advised.

"And how's *that*?" Ellis said.

Jo Nell crossed over to admire the tree, examining each ornament as if she'd never seen them before. "How pretty!" she exclaimed, fingering a fragile glass bird. "Where did you find this one, Lucy Nan?"

"Jo Nell Touchstone! You gave it to me yourself when you drew my name last year," I reminded her.

All of us were laughing when Idonia and Melrose made their entrance, somewhat hesitantly, through the dining room from the kitchen, so I suppose we did present sort of a laid-back front.

"It was much easier coming in the back way," Idonia said, slipping out of a tan suede jacket I'd never seen before, and I'll swear she looked as if she'd lost at least five pounds! Melrose, of course, was at her side to receive it, along with her muffler, hat, and gloves. "I'd like all of you to meet my friend, Melrose DuBois," she said, beginning introductions all around.

I stepped up to relieve Melrose of his burdens and welcome him to my home, and after a few minutes of awkward chatter, Ben and some of the other men whisked him away to the kitchen. That devil Ellis Saxon smiled at me from across the room, and I turned quickly away to steer Idonia toward the refreshments. The two of us had discussed earlier what we expected Melrose to look like, and I'll be darned if he didn't fit the description down to his holiday bow tie and trim mustache!

A good four inches shorter than Idonia, who towered over him at five feet nine, Melrose DuBois was a round sturdy man with ruddy cheeks and a fringe of graying brown hair, who looked as if he might have stepped right out of the early nineteen hundreds. If he had plucked a pipe from inside his coat and sported a pocket watch, I wouldn't have been a bit surprised.

While the others gathered around Idonia with assurances of her new friend's welcome, I found a spot on the table for her fruit tray and put a cup of hot punch in her hand. Idonia doesn't care for alcohol, but she has finally gotten used to seeing the rest of us indulge now and then.

"He's every bit as nice as you said he was," Claudia said. "And so polite, too."

"And such a pleasant smile," Nettie added. "I'll bet he has a good sense of humor."

I agreed with Zee that Idonia's gentleman friend was a brave soul to take on all of us at once, and Idonia seemed to relax and bask in the glow of the pleasantries. And pleasantries were what they were. Melrose DuBois didn't have the charm of a Cary Grant, the wit of a Robin Williams, or the sex appeal of a George Clooney—but then, who does? He was simply a Melrose, through and through, and if that was enough for Idonia Mae Culpepper, it was enough for me.

Tonight Idonia wore a sea green turtleneck tunic with beige wool pants and brown suede fur-trimmed boots. The gold locket with the two missing seed pearls glowed softly against her sweater. I don't think she'd gone out without it since Melrose gave it to her a few days before.

Later, as we left to go caroling, I saw Augusta for just an instant out of the corner of my eye as she stood in the hallway wrapping herself in her "forty miles" of cape before stepping outside with the carolers. She pulled a plum-colored hat over her radiant hair before disappearing from my vision completely.

Everyone else was bundled to the teeth as well. In fact, most of us wore so many layers it was hard to tell one person from another. Claudia's husband Brian, who claimed to be tone deaf, elected to stay and keep the home fires burning, but the rest of us waddled out looking like so many penguins. "If I fall, promise you won't let me roll away," I said to Ben as we maneuvered the front steps together. He pressed my gloved hand close against him as we started out. "Just try and get away," he whispered, making me feel warmer at once.

"Where to?" called Ellis, who, with Bennett and Weigelia, led the way.

"Why not start with the Johnsons next door?" Zee answered, throwing the beam of her flashlight along the low stone wall that led to our neighbor's house.

Our neighbors huddled politely in the doorway listening to our rendition of "Oh, Come All Ye Faithful," and even braved the cold to hear a couple of verses of "Jingle Bells." We declined their invitation to come in for eggnog and fruitcake and hurried along to the next house. Melrose's tenor, we discovered, blended beautifully with Ben's baritone, so we urged the two of them to the front of the group with Weigelia after that. Augusta, I noticed, stood at a discreet distance mouthing the words, and I ached for her, knowing how she wanted to sing.

Since they both sang alto, Idonia dropped back to stand next to Nettie at the rear of the carolers, but her eyes were only for

Melrose, and the pride in her face was obvious as she listened to him sing.

"Couldn't we just skip the Willoughbys?" Zee asked as we hurried across the street. "You know good and well Myrtle will pass around those awful cookies."

"I don't know how we can ignore them," Ellis told her. "Besides, you don't have to take one."

But that, we found, was easier said than done. "I'm so glad you came around tonight—been baking all afternoon!" Myrtle Willoughby quickly threw a wrap about her. "Quick, Wilbur, bring me the cookie jar! I have plenty for everybody," she called, hurrying to meet us. "Now, don't be shy…take two—more if you like." She shoved the container at each of us in turn. "Now, don't tell me you're dieting," she said to Zee. "Nobody diets at Christmastime."

"I'm glad we didn't sing that song about the figgy pudding," Paul Touchstone commented as we left. "She might've made some of that, too!"

Ben burst forth with his booming laugh. "That reminds me of this little maiden lady who lived over in Sweet Gum Valley, where I grew up," he began. "Seems she was interested in the new preacher in town, and somebody told her they'd heard the fellow liked a woman with a big mouth... so she invited him over for dinner. 'Won't you have some HAM, TATERS, and APPLE PIE?' she said, stretching her mouth as large as she could. Well, that didn't do the trick," he continued when the laughter died down, "so she reckoned he must favor the opposite. Well, the next time he came to dinner she made up her mind not to open her mouth any bigger than a keyhole. 'Preacher,' she said, 'help yourself to some of them prunes, and please pass the pudding.'"

Nettie prodded him with her flashlight. "Do law, Ben Maxwell, I believe you made that up!"

"Did *not*! It was one of those McGaritys—Ruby Lee, I think

it was—lived just down the road from my grandmama—ugly as homemade sin, the lot of them!"

We had decided to serenade the last two families on the block and call it a night, and were congregating on the Dorseys' front walk when somebody jostled me from the rear and I turned to find Idonia practically breathing down my neck.

"Jo Nell, will you please stop crowding me? You're stepping on my heels," she complained.

"I don't know how, since I'm standing over here," Jo Nell said from a couple of feet away.

"Well, somebody keeps bumping into me. I can't take a step without being shoved from behind," Idonia insisted.

"Don't look at me," Nettie said. I noticed that she had moved up beside Claudia and Zee in an effort to move things along. "Let's sing 'Rudolph,' that's a lively one," she said, beating her mittened hands together.

"How about 'The Twelve Days of Christmas'?" Bennett joked.

"And how about we leave you here to sing a solo?" Ellis suggested.

My feet were so numb I could hardly feel them as we sang "Deck the Halls" to Amelia Kimbrough at the house on the corner, ending with "Silent Night," and if I hadn't been so cold, I could have listened to more. The voices of Ben, Melrose, and Weigelia, with others blending in harmony, were so sweet it brought tears to my eyes. I quickly wiped them away before they could freeze on my face and walked ahead of the others to get a start on warming the soup and pastries.

Idonia caught up with me as I hurried up the front walk. "Lucy Nan, I think somebody's been following me," she said, panting to keep up.

"You mean tonight? Idonia, we were all out there together. It was probably just somebody in our group."

She glanced behind her as we went inside together. "I thought so, too, at first, but the whole time we were caroling, I heard footsteps a few steps behind me, and once, when we sang at the Dorseys', I'm sure somebody tried to grab my arm."

"Are you sure it wasn't Melrose?" I smiled, trying to make light of the situation, but Idonia wasn't amused.

"You know good and well he was with Ben and Weigelia. He wasn't even near me!"

"Were you able to get a look at this person at all?" I asked, thinking it was probably Nettie or one of the others.

In the kitchen, Idonia slipped out of her coat and tossed her gloves onto a chair. "Everybody was so bundled up, it was hard to tell who was who, but I really don't think it was one of us. Whoever it was had a scarf wrapped over his face, and whenever I turned around, he seemed to move away. I'm sure I saw somebody slip into the shadows of that big magnolia in the Dorseys' front yard."

"But why? What do you think they wanted?"

"I can't imagine, but it made me feel uncomfortable, and, Lucy Nan, you know me well enough to know I'm not easily excitable." She peeked inside the slow cooker. "Mm…soup smells good! Butternut squash?"

I nodded. Upon our return to the house we had found our fire keeper, Brian, watching a football game in the sitting room while the fire burned to ashes on the living-room hearth. Somehow, I noticed, Augusta had managed to slip back inside and turn up the heat on the cooker, and checking the oven, I found foil-wrapped meat pastries warm and ready to serve.

Voices and laughter in the living room alerted us the others had returned, and Idonia drew me aside as we went to greet them. "I'd rather you not mention this to Melrose, Lucy Nan. I don't want him to think I'm one of those hysterical women who gets upset over nothing."

I gave her a reassuring hug. "I won't," I said, "and you aren't."

In the living room a shamefaced Brian added wood to the fire and Nettie settled into the closest chair to pull off her boots and warm her feet. "I'm not moving," she announced, "until I can feel my toes again."

With Weigelia's help I set out trays of pastries and mugs of soup to have with the fruit Idonia had brought earlier, and Ellis arranged a huge platter of cookies, jam cake, and lemon bars for dessert. Seated on the sofa, Idonia, her cheeks still flushed from the cold, laughed with Melrose at something Bennett was telling them.

"Remember the first time we were served vichyssoise?" Bennett said, winking at Ellis.

Ellis made a face. "How could I forget when you keep reminding me?" She laughed. "We were just out of college," she explained, "and were invited to a progressive supper. The first course was vichyssoise served like this—in mugs." She glanced at Bennett, who took up the story.

"It was cold, of course, with chives sprinkled on top, and neither of us had ever had it before…" Bennett waited for a signal from his wife before continuing. "On the way home, I asked Ellis how she liked the soup, and she said she reckoned it was okay once you got used to the cold, but she had an awful time straining those pine needles through her teeth!"

"Idonia tells us you're staying over at the Spring Lamb," Paul Touchstone said to Melrose, after the laughter died down. "Getting enough to eat over there?" he added, ignoring his wife's warning frown.

Melrose patted his round stomach and laughed. "Obviously, I'm getting enough somewhere, but I take most of my meals out."

"Working over at the funeral home, I guess you get the news firsthand when anybody around here dies," Zee said.

Melrose nodded solemnly. "Sooner or later, that's where we all end up, only I'd a whole lot rather it be later."

Nettie washed a lemon bar down with coffee. "I don't reckon Joe Harris Carlisle's been around lately?"

"Joe Harris Carlisle...?" Melrose looked puzzled at the laughter that followed. "Don't believe I've met the fellow."

"You will," Nettie told him. "Comes in every so often to get measured for his coffin."

"Must weigh over three hundred pounds," Zee explained, "and just keeps on getting bigger, so Joe Harris has Al Evans measure him now and then just to be sure he'll fit."

"That's right," Weigelia told him as she helped herself to coffee. "And there ain't no way you be missing him when he comes in, either."

Claudia laughed. "If I don't stop eating, I'm afraid I'll be in the same fix! These pies are wonderful, Lucy Nan. Where do you get all these great recipes?"

"Must be heaven sent," Ellis said from across the room, and I could plainly see Augusta standing beside her. The two of them were obviously enjoying their little joke.

"It was a very nice party," Augusta said after everyone left. "Everyone seemed to enjoy the caroling and the singing was lovely. Your friends are fortunate to be blessed with such lovely voices."

"I know," I said, putting the last plate in the dishwasher. "It was fun, wasn't it?"

Augusta gave the dog a treat. Poor Clementine had been banished upstairs for the duration of the party and was now basking in the attention being showered upon her. "I'm afraid I didn't last long enough to hear most of it," Augusta admitted, teasing Clementine with a dog biscuit under her apron. "As you know, I'm not fond of the cold."

I nodded. "Did you last long enough to notice if someone was following Idonia?"

"Following Idonia? Why, no, I didn't see anyone, but then everyone had on so many wraps, it would have been difficult to tell them apart."

Augusta rewarded Clementine with the biscuit and went to the closet for the broom. I watched in amazement as she twirled it about the floor in so many loops and whirls, before putting it back in its place. After all the guests who had passed through our kitchen that night, not a crumb or a speck of dirt remained. "I wish I could do that. Do you think you could teach me?" I joked.

But Augusta didn't smile. "Why does Idonia believe someone was following her?"

"She has no idea, but she was truly frightened, and she isn't the high-strung type."

"I did notice one thing that rather bothers me," Augusta said. "That locket Idonia was wearing—the one shaped like a flower—is exactly like the one the Tanseys' daughter wore in that photograph on their piano."

NINE

"ARE YOU ABSOLUTELY SURE?" Ellis asked Augusta the next day. "Could you really tell that much about a photograph? Maybe Idonia's locket isn't absolutely identical to the one Dinah Tansey wore."

"There could be several like that," I said. "How do we know the Tansey girl had the only one of its kind?" Unlike Augusta, I hadn't paid much attention to the locket in the photograph and held on to the hope that Melrose DuBois wasn't a liar and that our good friend wouldn't be hurt because of him.

Augusta continued putting away dishes from last night's party and her silence seemed to go on forever. When she spoke, her voice was so soft I had to move closer to hear. "The seed pearls are missing in the same places," she said, turning to face us. "I'm sorry, but it seems that something's not right."

Ellis had dropped by after church that Sunday to collect her chafing dish and had surprised us with a huge red poinsettia for the dining room. "I would've brought it in time for the party yesterday, but I don't know where you'd have put it with all that food," she said.

Frowning now, she traced with her finger the Z-shaped scratch on my kitchen table where Roger had tried to build a picture frame from scrap lumber for his Boy Scout project. "So where did Melrose get the locket he gave Idonia? You don't suppose he stole it, do you?" Her face turned almost as red as the plant she brought. "And I was beginning to like him, too!"

Augusta spoke calmly. "Let's not accuse anyone until we know the truth. No purpose is ever served by hopping over the firearm."

Ellis rolled her eyes at me and shrugged. "Jumping the gun," I mouthed when Augusta wasn't looking.

"Isn't Claudia supposed to visit the Tanseys this afternoon to help deliver that fruitcake?" I said. "Maybe we can catch her before they leave."

"That chicken! I knew she'd let Opal Henshaw browbeat her into going, but now I'm glad she did." Ellis reached for the phone. "I'll give her a call and ask her to try and get a good look at that photograph."

"Just tell her not to mention it to Opal," I reminded her. "The less she knows about this, the better."

"Didn't you say the police planned to have another look around your grandmother's old home?" Augusta asked while Ellis made her phone call. "I wonder if they'll discover anything."

"Captain Hardy said he'd let me know if something turned up, but if I don't hear from him by tomorrow, I'll give him a call," I said. "There was a small mention about the man falling from the balcony in the Columbia paper today, but it still didn't identify him as Dexter Clark."

Augusta looked thoughtful. "Perhaps the authorities aren't ready to release the man's identity."

"They must have a reason for keeping it quiet," I said.

Ellis finished her phone call and told us that Opal planned to come by for Claudia promptly at two o'clock to deliver their Christmas baskets. "Poor Claudia!" she said. "It's probably going to take them most of the afternoon. Can you imagine spending all afternoon with Opal Henshaw?"

"You did remind her to make a point to look at that photograph, didn't you?" I asked her.

"I reminded, and Claudia promised. Let's just hope she isn't too obvious about it."

"Well?" I asked Ellis later that day when she came over to dress for Bellawood's candlelight tour. "Have you heard anything from Claudia?"